in a HEARTBEAT

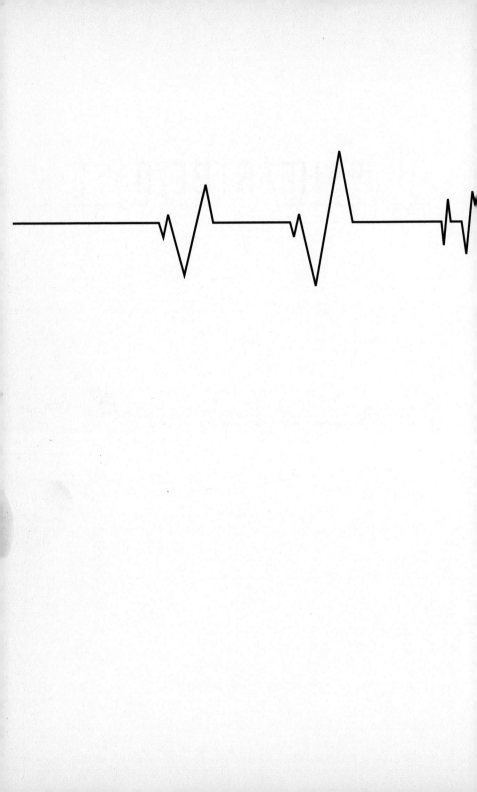

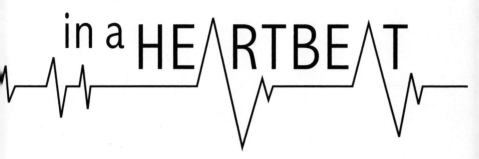

in a HEARTBEAT

LORETTA ELLSWORTH

Walker & Company ✺ New York

First published in the United States of America in February 2010 by
Walker Publishing Company, Inc., a division of Bloomsbury Publishing, Inc.
Visit Walker & Company's Web site at www.bloomsburyteens.com

For information about permission to reproduce selections from this book, write to
Permissions, Walker & Company, 175 Fifth Avenue, New York, New York 10010

Library of Congress Cataloging-in-Publication Data
Ellsworth, Loretta.
In a heartbeat / Loretta Ellsworth.
   p.   cm.
Summary: Told in their separate voices, Eagan, who has died in a figure-skating accident, becomes
a heart donor for Amelia, who then begins taking on some aspects of Eagan's personality.
ISBN: 978-0-8027-2068-9
[1. Heart—Transplantation—Fiction. 2. Donation of organs, tissues, etc.—Fiction.
3. Death—Fiction. 4. Personality—Fiction.] I. Title.
PZ7.E4783Imt 2010   [Fic]—dc22   2009019196

Book design by Danielle Delaney
Typeset by Westchester Book Composition
Printed in the U.S.A. by Quebecor World Fairfield, Pennsylvania
2 4 6 8 10 9 7 5 3 1

All papers used by Walker & Company are natural, recyclable products
made from wood grown in well-managed forests. The manufacturing processes
conform to the environmental regulations of the country of origin.

In memory of my nephew
Jason Mennen (1985–2005), an organ donor

I went to sleep; and now I am refreshed.
A strange refreshment: for I feel in me
An inexpressive lightness, and a sense
Of freedom, as I were at length myself
And ne'er had been before.

—Cardinal John Henry Newman

EAGAN

I'm fatalistic. I've always had the feeling that time was running out. After 9/11, I started reading end-of-the-world-type books: *Alas, Babylon; Lucifer's Hammer; On the Beach; The Stand.* Then I started hoarding bottles of water and granola bars under my bed. Last year I spent my birthday money on two hundred batteries, which I kept in a shoe box at the back of my closet.

Of course, I never intended to die. I mean, really die. I thought I'd be one of those who *survived* the end-of-the-world catastrophe. In the end, what did me in was a freak accident. No end of the world, just the end of my world. If I had to do it all over again, I'd have eaten those granola bars.

The odd part is that the whole thing started in such a small way.

I was off by an inch. No, less than that. Half an inch. The size of a shirt button. Hardly worth mentioning. Most people barely notice half an inch. Except for my geometry teacher, who made us estimate to the nearest *quarter* inch. Mrs. Koster said accuracy was of the utmost importance.

But it's not. Not always. Like the curb I backed onto last month when I was parallel parking for my driver's license test. I'd swerved too sharply and the back tire of Mom's blue Chevy slid half an inch off the pavement. I swallowed hard, thinking how embarrassed I would be when I had to tell everyone that I flunked. I thought of Mom watching from the redbrick building across the road, of the disappointment I'd have to see on her face. I thought my life was over right then and there.

But the nice man with the bushy brows said that mistake only reduced my score by five points. Not enough to fail me. Half an inch didn't keep me from getting my driver's license.

In gym class when I threw the basketball, if I aimed at the center of the net, half an inch didn't make a bit of difference. The ball still went through the hoop.

Half an inch. Slightly less than the diameter of a dime.

Most of the time I wouldn't even have noticed if I was half an inch off. Even in figure skating, half an inch can be covered up. If you move half an inch on your sit spin, you might not even get a deduction.

But sometimes half an inch is *really* important. If your timing is off and you miss your triple lutz landing, you could end up on your butt on the cold ice. Or worse, you could do what I did. You could go flying off into the boards and hit your head on the edge, a tiny half inch of sharp white board, and if you hit it just right like I did, you die.

Half an inch. It's enough to cause dreams to fall apart, enough to make the difference between life and death.

I should have listened to Mrs. Koster when she told us what a difference half an inch could make.

Amelia

I sat cross-legged on the gray carpet of my bedroom floor drawing a picture of a horse, absorbed in the details of the horse's head. The eyelashes weren't right. They were too long. Too feminine. He was a stallion, after all.

I glanced up as a stallion on TV snorted. A man yanked on the reins and the horse turned around. They sprinted off into the sunset, leaving a haze of trail dust in their wake.

I didn't notice Mom right away. She was at the door, her whole body rigid, gripping the doorknob. When I looked up, she reminded me of Kyle's little car when it's wound tight, just before he lets it zoom across the floor. And I knew what it was even before she opened her mouth. I knew something big was about to happen.

"The beeper went off," I said.

Mom nodded. Her voice was rushed. "We have to leave right away. Aunt Sophie is coming over to watch Kyle. Your dad is going to meet us there."

Her eyes held mine for a long moment. I nodded and held

back tears. For weeks I'd imagined how it would be when Mom told me, how I thought I'd feel. I'd pictured myself jumping up and down in excitement, both of us bursting into happy tears. Two months of waiting. People die every day waiting for the call. Now I was one of the lucky ones.

But in that instant I couldn't think of luck or happiness. I froze, trapped in that moment, afraid to speak.

A commercial for batteries came on. I turned my head and watched as the Energizer Bunny zoomed back and forth. I would have run out of power halfway across the screen. I didn't have the energy to jump up and down with excitement. Every morning I woke up tired.

Mom finally sprang to action. She reached down and yanked my packed suitcase out of the bedroom corner with shaking hands. Her mouth trembled.

"Is there anything else you need to pack? Do you want to put your notebook and drawing pencils in here?"

My fingers grasped a brown pencil. My fingertips were blue and chubby, as if they'd already accepted the lack of oxygen and were hibernating. I listened to the beat, the sound of my heart, swishing like a washing machine. Was it possible that sound would go away? That I'd stop feeling like I was carrying a stack of books on my chest and be able to walk down the steps in my own house?

A picture of me sits on my dresser. I'm posing with my soccer team when I was eight, before I got sick. The girl in the picture is as strange to me as the photos of my dead grandmother. I'm supposed to remember her, but I don't.

"Drawing pencils?" Mom reminded me, her hand outstretched.

I held out the pack to her. "What if it doesn't fit?" I said, my left hand covering my heart as if I were pledging allegiance.

"Oh, there's plenty of room in here . . . ," she started, but then stopped. Mom looked at me hard, like she looks when she's working her crossword. Finally she reached over and touched the side of my face. "I have a feeling about this, honey."

"Okay." I swallowed. Mom knew I was sick before I knew it myself. She has a sixth sense about that stuff.

I closed my notebook filled with horses. They're all I draw—horses. The only thing I've ever drawn since I was little. The only thing that relaxes me. Arabians, Morgans, Thoroughbreds, Palominos. I've researched them all: their anatomy and muscles and bones, the different breeds, how the light shades their faces. I've ridden one once, a mare the color of the clay pots outside my window, cinnamon and rust. Her name was Dusty.

I was about to turn off the TV when the news came on. They were reporting on an accident on Interstate 35. I stopped and stared, hoping that wasn't where my heart was coming from. The last few months I'd paid closer attention to the news, listening for the ages of victims, wondering if they died on the spot or at the hospital, wondering if the doctors saved their hearts.

I didn't want to live through another person's death. But it was part of the deal. Dr. Michael had said, "People are going to die regardless of whether you live or not. Their gift to you might help ease the pain of the family and friends who are mourning that person's loss."

But the fact remained that someone else had to die for me to live. Someone else had to grieve for me to be happy. And every night at dinner, when my family prayed for a new heart for me, we were praying for that to happen.

3

EAGAN

The only funeral I ever attended was Grandma's. She looked like she was asleep in her favorite purple dress. Mom said Grandma was looking down on us from heaven, which gave me the creeps.

I think I'm dead. Really dead, as in no longer on Earth. I feel removed from my body, like a balloon that someone let loose and is floating up into the ozone. I'm in nowhere land, a gray misty place. The gray is thick like fog, but it's dry and has no texture or substance. I try to push through it, but it's like pushing through water—more fog fills in the gap. If I am dead, I hope I don't have to stay here forever. I hate gray. I'm more of a purple person, like Grandma.

"Help!" I shout. No one answers. I feel alone and it scares me. I don't want to be here. I want to be back on the ice, finishing my performance. Or at home in my bed, having a bad dream. Or even in the hospital, drugged up and hurt, with a bad headache, but still alive.

The only thing keeping me from screaming is that my life is playing out in bits and pieces in front of me. You know how when people on TV die, their lives flash before their eyes? That's kind of how it is for me. Fragments of my life are laid out in front of me like an interactive photo album. All I have to do is remember a moment and there it all is. Every detail!

Of course, right now all I can focus on are the negative moments. Some things don't change with death. I'm starting with the last meal I ate, my own personal Last Supper.

—╱╲ᵥ—

"Eat your meat," Mom ordered. I was picking through my chicken. I'd found a pink spot and I couldn't stand eating chicken that was even a tiny bit pink. But Mom was watching me. She had tried out another new recipe: chicken cacciatore, which had tomatoes in it. Maybe that's what was making the chicken look pink, but I still didn't want to eat it.

I made a face at Dad, who was chomping away. He could eat anything. I ate more pasta.

Mom put down her napkin. "You're not becoming anorexic, are you? You're awfully thin."

I rolled my eyes. "No, Mom. You see me eat all the time."

"A lot of figure skaters have that problem. How do I know you're not one of them?"

I picked at my chicken. That's what she sounded like: a chicken clucking. The senseless noise irritated my ears.

"Not our Eagan," Dad reassured her. "She eats all the time. She just aced her physical." Dad patted his round stomach. "She's thin because she inherited your genes, Cheryl."

Mom always said she'd been fighting off the same twenty-five pounds ever since I was born. Now she smiled at the compliment. I took a drink of milk to hide my smirk.

"Keep eating, Eagan," she told me.

I sighed and picked at the chicken. How could she *not* know that I ate? And I *did* ace my physical after throwing a fit when Mom tried to follow me into the exam room.

"Dr. Joyce let me listen to my heart through the stethoscope, Dad. She said I had a low heart rate, like a trained athlete. She's so much better than old Dr. Peterson too." I'd listened for the first time to my heart beating in my chest, the thump-thump of my own percussion section.

"You always loved Dr. Peterson when you were little," Mom said.

Dad smiled. "Well, she's not little anymore. She's growing up into a young woman. In a couple of years she'll be off to college."

"Or maybe in two years she'll be competing at the senior level. Maybe she'll want to see how far she can go in skating first."

"Hello? Isn't that up to me to decide? It is *my* future, after all."

Dad stuck his fork into another piece of chicken. "Of course, pumpkin. We just want what's best for you."

Mom reached over with her fork and knife and cut my chicken into smaller chunks. "We know how hard you've worked. We know how much talent you have."

"I'm not two years old." I pulled my plate away from her. "And I don't like to eat a lot before a competition. That doesn't make me anorexic like . . ." I stopped before the name popped out.

"Like who?"

I fiddled with my fork. "None of your business."

"Eagan, you lose that attitude this instant. Anorexia is a serious sickness. Is this girl getting help?"

"Yes."

"Well, who is it?"

I leaned over and looked out the window. Where was Kelly? I needed saving. My packed bag and skates sat ready in the foyer.

"Eagan," Mom persisted.

"Okay, okay. Just stop bugging me. It's Bailey."

It wasn't often that I could surprise Mom. She was reaching for her water and almost knocked the glass over. "Bailey? But she's . . ."

"A little heavy? Our coaches have told us all about anorexia and bulimia, Mom. You don't have to be überthin to have it."

"Well, I'm just flabbergasted. I thought she was trimming down so she could make her jumps better."

"Do her parents know?" Dad looked up from his plate but didn't stop eating.

"Yeah. She's getting therapy, but the coaches might not let her compete for a while."

"What about Nationals?" Mom's voice sounded hopeful. I suspected the hope wasn't out of concern for Bailey.

"It's up to the coaches."

"But you're the first alternate."

"I know, Mom."

Mom clapped her hands together. "I have to get time off work. Nationals. Colorado!"

I tried not to get caught up in her excitement. Sure, I wanted to go to Nationals. If Bailey had accidentally torn a ligament or something, that'd be fine. But not this way. It would be kicking Bailey when she was already down.

No way would I eat a bite of Mom's chicken now. She claimed she wasn't one of those pushy skating moms, that she was diligent when it came to making an investment of time and money. I could quit whenever I wanted. But if I wanted to skate, I had to do it *her* way. In ten years she never let me skip a practice. She watched at least one practice a week and my coach was on her speed dial.

I stretched my legs under the table. I hated this glass table, hated how everything underneath was visible. Mom's feet folded at the ankles and tucked under her chair. Dad's brown loafers tapped the floor as he ate, as if he couldn't wait to be done. I couldn't even flip Mom off under the table. She'd see.

What if I dumped my plate off the edge? How would that look through the glass?

I peeked at Mom. She was frowning at me as if she knew my thoughts, so I distracted her by pointing at the lighted candles. "What's the special occasion? The last time you lit the candles was Easter dinner."

Mom's eyes were different shades of brown that changed depending on her mood. Now they held a copper tint as she flashed a quick look at Dad. He raised one eyebrow at her. The bald patch on the top of his head glistened in the candlelight.

"We have something to tell you," Mom said, playing with her napkin under the table as she spoke. "It's about the trip Dad and I took to Hawaii."

The trip where I had to stay with Grandpa and rake wet leaves into a garbage bag instead of sunning on the warm beaches of Maui? The trip where there had been lots of fighting beforehand, and Dad said it would help their marriage? "The trip you took for your marriage problems," I said.

"Well, I'd call it more of a vacation," Mom said, blushing.

"Then why didn't I get to go?"

"We needed time to ourselves, Eagan."

"I would have left you alone if you'd taken me."

"You had practice. Besides, we needed to get away."

"From me?"

"For God's sake, Eagan, it isn't always about you."

"You're right. It's always about *you*."

Mom sighed and shook her head. "You know what? Just forget it."

Yes, please. I didn't need this before a competition.

I felt grouchy, ready to fight again. I hadn't slept well, but I didn't dare mention that I was tired. Not after they'd caught Scott in my room last night when they'd returned from the movies. Not after I'd argued with Mom and confronted her with her lies. Not after she'd found my stash of bottles and granola bars and had yelled at me and said she'd take me to a therapist if I didn't change my outlook.

"Hey, now." Dad put down his fork. "I don't want my two girls fighting during dinner. Eagan, parents go on vacation without their kids all the time. It's not a crime."

"Yeah, sure." I didn't care if they went away without me. I'd just wanted to go to Hawaii.

Mom jutted out her chin like she was getting ready to yell, but then she reached over and pulled my plate back, away from the edge of the table. "So tell me more about Bailey. How long do you think she'll be out? I'll have to say something to Barbara. Poor woman." I could see her brain working, coming up with something sympathetic to say, even while planning how I would take Bailey's place at Nationals.

"I'm sorry for Bailey, but she's always been kind of nasty to you. Remember three years ago when she had a sleepover and didn't invite you, and you cried the whole evening? Plus, Bailey doesn't have the total package. You do. That's why you can go far in this sport."

"Mom, just because you skated a million years ago doesn't make you an expert. And Bailey's a lot nicer now."

"Your coach is the one who always tells me how talented you are. I hate to say it, but Bailey has legs like tree trunks. And starving herself isn't going to make her beautiful like you."

I wished Mom was more like Dad. He still didn't know the difference between an axel and a sit spin.

"Maybe Bailey will be allowed to compete," I said in a positive voice. "Her coach wants her to continue practicing."

Mom shook her head. "How can they allow that? Someone should talk to them."

I pushed back my chair. "God, Mom. It's none of your business. I shouldn't even have told you about Bailey."

"I'm just thinking of Bailey, of what's best for her."

I glared at her. "No, you're not. You're thinking of getting her disqualified so I can go to Nationals instead of her."

Mom put her hand on her throat. "What an awful thing to say."

A car horn blared outside. My ride was here.

Mom looked at me as though I was a stranger. I stood and grabbed my skates and bag. "Awful words for an awful person," I said.

Amelia

The beeper had gone off. What I'd hoped for but dreaded. I could hear Mom downstairs, putting in a hurried load of laundry, the water rushing through the pipes. It reminded me of Dr. Michael, of how he always washed his hands before he touched me, how he tapped his knuckles on the sink to get off the excess water, then patted them dry on a paper towel.

"You're in the early stages of CHF, congestive heart failure. It's time to start thinking about a heart transplant." Dr. Michael had folded his arms the way he always did when he talked to me. His voice softened too.

"Can't you just fix my heart?"

He'd patted my back. I liked the gentle way he touched me, like I was a porcelain doll, an expensive doll that might break if handled without care.

"Sorry, kiddo. We've done all we can. A transplant is the way to go now. We've come a long way in the last six years. We're going to do better than just fix that worn-out heart. We're going to get you a new one."

But I hadn't wanted a new one. I'd wanted my old one fixed.

Dr. Michael's nurse had given me a book written by a kid who'd had a heart transplant. The cover showed him skiing down the Alps afterward, wearing a shiny yellow alpine jacket over his new heart, his rosy cheeks flushed with good health. Mom and Dad had gotten a bunch of pamphlets too, including one called *Teens and Heart Transplants*.

I'd stared at the book. Was that boy really as happy and healthy as he looked? How did he feel about having someone else's heart in him?

"And remember," Dr. Michael had said before we left, "write down any questions you have so you can ask me next time."

I'd written one question a week: How long would the operation take? Would it hurt? How long would my new heart last? What would they do with my old heart?

Dr. Michael had answered each one. He didn't laugh. He didn't say they were dumb questions. He'd said that the operation usually takes several hours, that I'd be asleep and wouldn't feel anything, and that they didn't know how long my heart would last, but if I took my medication it could last my whole lifetime. He'd said my old heart would be disposed of.

After talking with him, I would feel better for the rest of the day, until another question popped up, another worry that I carried around until the following week. Another weight on my already heavy heart.

Slowly I learned about the procedure. The transplant team would be checking out my donor heart while I was getting ready for surgery. I'd wake up with a tube in my mouth and a catheter in my bladder and tubes draining from my chest. With someone else's heart inside me.

I was more worried about the tube in my mouth at first. The thought of not being able to talk to Mom or Dad scared me. What if something hurt? How would I tell them?

"You'll have something to write on," Dr. Michael had said.

I'd had a catheter before. I *knew* that hurt.

"We'll take it out as soon as we can," Dr. Michael had said. "And you'll be on pain medication, so you won't feel it like before."

Now I sat on my bedroom floor, playing that moment over in my mind, wishing I could freeze time or even move it back to before the beeper went off. It wasn't so bad, living this way, even though I was getting worse.

First had come the low-salt diet. Not so bad, but I missed pizza and popcorn. Then came all the medicine, even the one that made my face swell. I couldn't go to school, couldn't face the staring. I stayed in my room most of the time because I looked like a chipmunk. Later came the hacking cough and the diuretics that made me go to the bathroom all the time. By then I was being homeschooled. No school field trips. No parties. No friends.

Worst of all, the shortness of breath. At first I couldn't run. Then I couldn't make it up the steps to my bedroom. The wheelchair at the mall made me feel like a freak.

And the last resort was the transplant list. I was still alive, but how long would I last? And how long had it been since I'd felt like a normal person? Even if I got a new heart, did I remember how to live anymore?

I stared down at my half-finished drawing, until I noticed Kyle peeking around the corner of my door. He held a pack of cards in his sticky hands. His sweaty blond bangs stuck to his forehead like frosting dripping down the side of a cake.

"What you doin'?"

Mom called Kyle a hurricane in motion. I called him a spoiled brat. Even though Mom had taken my pencils, I hid behind my notebook, scared and nervous, but not wanting to admit it to my kid brother.

"Drawing."

"With what? You don't have anything to draw with."

"I'm *thinking* of what to draw."

"Wanna play cards?"

"I'm busy."

"Aunt Sophie's going to take me to a ninja movie tomorrow, and we're going to order pizza too."

"That's nice."

"Mom said I gotta wait two or three days after you get your new heart to come visit."

His voice was light. Mom and Dad hadn't told him how serious the surgery was. They said seven was too young to understand, so they sugarcoated it like they used to do for me, telling me I was going to get a pinch in the arm when it turned out to be a needle.

"I know," I replied. "Only Mom and Dad can visit me at first, and they'll have to wear special masks."

"Will I get to wear one too?"

"Maybe."

"All right!"

How dumb and selfish he was, just wanting to wear a stupid mask.

"You have to wear a mask so I don't catch any germs from you and *die*."

Kyle's mouth dropped open. He stepped closer. "Mom said you're going to be better after you get your heart. Better than you are now."

"Yeah, but I'll have to take antirejection medicine for the rest of my life or I could *die*."

"What's antirection medicine?"

"Anti*rejection*. It's medicine that tricks my body into thinking the new heart belongs to me. But it's just a trick because it won't really be *my* heart."

"You already take lots of medicine."

"This is different."

Kyle squinted at me. "Are you scared?"

Huh. Maybe he wasn't so dumb.

I looked back down at my notebook. "I'm just not happy about having surgery." It was true. Not like anyone had asked me. I didn't want to go. I didn't want any of this, but I especially didn't want to have my heart ripped out of me.

Kyle was quiet for a second. "Mom said you're going to be fine."

My chest felt heavy and I let out a short breath. "Mom doesn't know everything."

"You *have* to be fine." Kyle's face was scrunched up like I'd just punched him in the stomach.

Mom appeared then, hurrying down the hallway. "Amelia, you should be downstairs. We have to leave within thirty minutes of the call."

The lines around Mom's face and mouth were deeper today. She used to run all the time and kept four trophies from her high school track team on the bookshelf in the living room. They're gone now.

Kyle let out a sigh. He knew only that his sister had a

heart problem, and she took lots of medicine and didn't go to school like other kids.

I put down my notebook. "I'll be right there, Mom."

After she left, I turned to Kyle. "I'm going to play a quick game of cards first."

5

EAGAN

I'm not hungry or tired or sore. But there's more to this mist than grayness. I feel as if I'm being watched. Maybe I'm in a coma. I mean, I'm surrounded by gray fog instead of standing in front of the pearly gates of heaven. And no one is here to greet me, not even Grandma. That should probably tell me something. But worst of all, I don't even care. Because if I really am dead, then I was cheated. I wasn't supposed to die this young. And if I'm in a coma I could be trapped here for the rest of my life, and that's not fair, either.

I wonder about the moment my skull crashed against that edge. I wonder if there was a lot of blood, if it stained the ice red until the Zamboni scraped off the layer of ice. Or did I have internal injuries and look like I was sleeping? Did Mom and Dad want to reach out and shake me, as though that would help me wake up?

Grandma's funeral was the only one I ever attended. If I'm dead, I don't want to see mine. I couldn't bear to see the grief I caused.

I turn and twist and move through the fog. I call out. My voice echoes in the gray distance, as though I'm shouting off the top of a tall cliff. No one answers. I'm completely alone, except for the flashbacks from my life, which play out in front of me no matter where I move.

I tell myself to stop looking back at my past. It's not like my life was so fascinating or anything. There were only sixteen years of it. But I can't help myself, just as I was drawn to those end-of-the-world books even as I was laying out perfect plans for my own Olympic future. It's ironic that when I was alive, all I thought about was death. And now all I can think about is my life.

I remember those last hours. The last hours of my life.

Kelly had her own car, a red Pontiac Grand Am with a tea green interior that looked black unless light was shining on it.

Even though Kelly was the worst driver I knew, everything about her car felt safe. Not to mention cool. Bucket seats. Leopard fabric–covered steering wheel. WMYX blaring out the latest hits. The smell of lavender, Kelly's scent. Or maybe the cool part was Kelly herself, and the fact that she was willing to be friends with a sophomore.

"What?" she asked when I slammed the car door.

"My mom."

Kelly tapped my skull. "Put her out of your head. Just think about the competition."

"I never let her get into my head."

Silence. Kelly was thinking.

"She's in your head a lot. And why are you working overtime to make senior level?"

"Not for *her*."

"Right." Kelly peeled out of the driveway. "You're taking ballet lessons and you do off-ice conditioning besides skating practice five times a week. And that's fine because you're good enough to have that Olympic dream. But only if you're doing it for yourself."

Kelly paused. Her voice was low. "Sometimes I wonder if you're doing all this for *her*."

"God, she's *such* a head case," I said. "Nothing I do pleases her anyway."

"At least *your* mom makes it to all your competitions. My mom is going to my sister's soccer tournament today."

"Yeah, but you *want* your mom to come."

Kelly handed me a purple lollipop, my usual precompetition snack. "Look at it this way. You have a bigger cheering section."

I unwrapped the lollipop and took a long lick. "She needs therapy."

"Don't all moms?"

"Believe me, she needs it more than most."

"I have an aunt who takes antidepressants. Maybe you can slip some in your mom's drink."

"That's a great idea."

"I was joking!"

"I wasn't."

"You're bad." Kelly laughed as she made a quick right turn. She snorted when she laughed and never cared who heard it. "I'm going to miss this next year. You ragging about your mom. I'm even going to miss skating every day. It's stuck in my system. Wish I was as good as you, though."

Kelly had weak ankles from repetitive strains. She skated because she loved it, nothing more.

"Won't you miss competing?" I asked.

"No. I'm not into fame and glory like you."

"Come on. It's not just that. I love the costumes and the music and being able to land a triple salchow and do things that other people can't do."

Kelly's hair wove tightly around her head and gathered into a braided bun on top. She scratched at her braids. "That's the difference between us. I get too scared. You're not afraid of anything."

I pulled my fingers through my ponytail. I wouldn't put my hair up until just before competition. Fussing with my hair and makeup was a ritual that helped with precompetition nerves. I thought of telling Kelly how afraid I was that there wasn't much time left, how I felt an eerie sense of urgency. But this wasn't the time for pessimism. "Not true. I get butterflies just like you before competing. But once the music starts, I'm in my zone on the ice."

"Cold ice. That's one thing I won't miss at six in the morning."

Kelly had it all planned out. She was going to Florida State to study physical therapy. The only plan I'd ever had was skating.

Mom kept a scrapbook of my skating career. Whenever I looked at it, I was amazed at how much time I'd spent skating, at how much it had consumed my life. I tried to figure it out once. I'd spent 14,560 hours skating. Six hundred days, adding up to 1.7 years straight. And I spent at least another 14,000 hours doing skating-related stuff, like picking out my costumes and buying new skates and traveling to competitions.

Recently I'd been questioning the whole dream. But I wasn't sure I *could* let it go. And even if I wanted to, how would I ever tell Mom? I'd grown up with Mom's voice in my head. How could I hear my own voice beneath the roar of hers?

I sighed. "It won't be as fun next year without you."

"I'll be back over Christmas break. Besides, we still have this year." She put out her fist and we bumped knuckles, our good-luck sign. "Tonight we're gonna kick some ass."

"I'm doing my triple lutz tonight."

"You'll stick it too, Dynamo," Kelly said with certainty. "You make that in competition and you'll blow the judges away."

I stuck out a purple tongue. "Call me Purple Dynamo."

She pulled into the parking lot of the ice arena, a brown brick building with a slanted roof and floor-to-ceiling windows. I'd grown up learning to skate here, fighting for ice time with the hockey teams. I put my hand up to my ear and fingered the edge of my sapphire earring. Like Michelle Kwan's gold dragon necklace, I have my own good-luck symbol. The earrings had belonged to my grandma and had passed down to me when she died.

We hurried inside, past the refreshment counter and the odor of hot dogs and popcorn. We made our way down to the level of the ice, where the refrigerant smell eased my butterflies. My coach was talking to another coach, and my warm-up group was already there. As we passed by, I waved at Jasmine, one of the younger skaters, who would be competing in the level below me. She just turned ten last week. I changed into my skating dress and did my makeup and hair. Then I laced up my boots for the practice session.

Whenever I get on the ice at a rink, the first thing I do is bend down and feel the ice. Most people would laugh at this. Ice is ice, right? But each rink has its own touch, its own heartbeat. I knew how this one felt, but I still bent down and touched it out of habit. Tonight the ice was strangely absent of feeling. It was just cold. I stood and shook off a shiver.

During warm-ups, I attempted my triple lutz twice. I fell the first time, then landed it after that. I ended up close to the boards.

"Watch for the boards," my coach, Brian, said. "They're behind you on the jump and they come up fast."

"Okay."

He shook his head. "I've never trained anyone as gutsy as you. Or as hyper. We should put rocks in your pockets to hold you down."

I twirled around. "Wouldn't work."

Tonight I was lucky. I was first in the competition, my short event. I'd get the combination jump out of the way at the top of my routine. Then I had the double axel and the triple lutz. After that, the remainder of my routine was a breeze. I pictured myself holding that first-place starburst trophy in my hands.

"You pumped?" Kelly asked me as I paced during the presentation of the judges. I tugged at my dress. It was plum silk with long mesh sleeves and gold rhinestone accents. The rhinestones reflected the overhead lights.

My hair is wild and hard to tame, but I'd pulled it into a tight bun with the help of lots of hair spray and a matching plum-colored scrunchie. Then I'd topped it off with glitter.

"Yeah. I love going first." This way, I wouldn't have to watch the other skaters landing their triple jumps before me, each success stabbing at my confidence. Fear and doubt were a skater's worst enemies, and I wasn't about to give in to them tonight.

My name was called.

"Don't think. Just skate," Brian told me. I skated out to the middle of the ice, stood stone-still in my pose. The overhead lights were hot and the ice was cold. I felt like a doll frozen in an action stance.

"Go, Dynamo!" Kelly and the other girls from my club yelled as I waited for the music to start. I'd chosen fast music, a *Pirates of the Caribbean* song that matched my daredevil personality.

I turned my head slightly and found Mom and Dad in their usual spot, third row up smack-dab in the middle of the rink. Dad was talking to a man next to him. Mom's hands were clasped together as if praying. Her eyes were bright and glowing. I felt ashamed for what I'd said—"Awful words for an awful person." I'd ruined dinner and had never found out what she'd wanted to talk about.

I caught Mom's eye just then. She smiled and waved at me. I gave her a small wave back.

Then I blocked out everything as I stared straight ahead. I got rid of the cheers, the voices, the rustling of programs. I even got rid of Mom.

The music began to play and my body responded on cue, each move choreographed. I glided across the ice and felt my silk dress flow away from my body. I swept around the perimeter of the ice, landed my combination jump in perfect time to the music, then gathered speed as the audience applauded.

I let the music seep through me and concentrated on each move. I could feel the adrenaline pumping. My heart raced.

I hit my double axel and circled around the rink toward the corner for the triple lutz. I launched off the back outside edge of my skate, which was what I was supposed to do, but I knew the minute my skates left the ice that I'd messed up somehow. I rose into the air and turned my body counterclockwise for three rotations. I was supposed to land on the outside edge of my opposite foot, but that's not what happened. When I came down, I was out of synch with my body, and the ice wasn't where it was supposed to be. I hit hard, landing on the wrong side of my skate. I tried to stop, tried to steady myself. I hit my toe pick on the ice and went flying. I was close to the boards. Too close. I had a fraction of a second, not enough time to move my head, but long enough to know I was going to hit the board. Long enough to know it would hurt.

6

Amelia

A car squealed in the driveway. I heard car doors open and slam shut, and then Aunt Sophie's familiar throaty voice, a sound I loved.

"It's a miracle. How wonderful," she yelled as she walked into the house. Then I heard Rachel call my name.

Kyle and I stared at each other above the cards. "Aunt Sophie and Rachel," we whispered in unison.

I dropped my cards and went to sit on my bed. The comforter was a gaudy yellow and orange. Mom bought it to make my room look brighter. I hugged my pillow close to my chest, wondering if I'd ever see my room again, my dresser and mirror, my white desk, the posters of horses.

I stared at a picture Mom had framed of a palomino pony I'd sketched running in a pasture, wondering at the wild eyes I'd drawn for him. I'm more of a packer horse, steady and dull. The kind of horse that tolerates almost anything and can be trusted to behave. But even packer horses get skittish sometimes. I wanted to burrow down into my bed, to nip at anyone who would make me move.

This was the only place I'd ever lived, at the end of a cul-de-sac in a quiet Minneapolis neighborhood. My window looked out at two pine trees in the backyard. I'd watched them grow over the years, watched the ice hang from their branches in winter and the birds disappear inside to hidden nests in summer. I'd drawn them, flanked by lots of horses. It was the only landscape I knew by heart.

Rachel burst into my room. She ran over and gave me a tight hug. Her long blond hair rubbed against my face. It smelled fruity and clean.

"I'm so happy for you, Amelia. Mom has been praying nonstop."

I wanted to get caught up in her happiness. Rachel made it sound like I'd won the lottery. The lottery of recycled hearts, and I was a lucky winner.

"I'm not ready," I confessed. "I'm not ready for this operation. I don't want to go, Rachel." I knew I sounded like a coward and a crybaby.

"Don't cry," she said, and she hugged me again, because now I really was crying. I didn't want to cry. I wanted to be happy like her, to be excited, the good kind of excitement that comes when wonderful things are happening, like when you win a new car. Not the excitement of winning a new heart.

Kyle still had the cards in his hand. His face was scrunched up again.

"I'll e-mail you every day and sneak up candy," Rachel assured me. "And next year, you'll be able to go to high school. You gotta try out for cheerleading."

If anyone could make me feel better, it was Rachel. Only Rachel could talk about cheerleading tryouts when I was going in for a heart transplant. I always wondered if she'd still be my friend if she weren't my cousin. She was so popular, and besides, most people don't want to be friends with a girl who's going to die.

"Cheerleading?" I said through my tears. "I can't even do a split."

"You can practice this summer. You already know the cheers."

Even if I weren't about to have a heart transplant, I knew I'd never be the cheerleading type. But I liked that Rachel saw that possibility in me. Her pink cheeks reminded me of Mom before she stopped running. When Rachel tied her long hair back, she kind of looked like a younger version of Mom.

"We have to go, Amelia," Mom yelled from downstairs.

Rachel sniffed back a tear. "We're all behind you, you know. You're not doing this on your own."

I took a small breath. Maybe if I got a new heart, I'd have new energy. But the thought of me jumping up and down doing cheers was too much to hope for. Could my body change that much?

It had been so long since I'd done normal things. Still, I could almost imagine myself as a regular girl, wearing cowboy boots and riding through tall prairie grass on a palomino pony just like the one in the picture. Playing a game of catch with Kyle in the backyard. Walking across the stage to accept my high school diploma, then going to art school. Maybe I could do those things. Maybe I could live.

Taking one last look at my room, I wiped my eyes. Kyle

looked at me, but he didn't say anything. Finally he stood up and gave me a hug.

"Have a good operation, Meely." Then he turned and ran to his room, kicking the cards from our game around the floor with his shoe.

I walked out of my room into the hallway. I'd always loved the way our maple staircase wound from the second floor to make a sweeping entrance to the living room of our house. But walking had become a big thing for me the last couple of years.

Dad had installed an electric chair along the railing of our staircase, a black vinyl chair that moved in slow motion. I called it the "electric chair" to scare Kyle. He was afraid at first, but later he stole rides in it when Mom wasn't watching. I used the chair all the time now. But it clanked down so slowly that Kyle could run down and up and down the steps again before I got to the bottom.

The chair had been the biggest change in our house. It was the final defeat. I never told Dad, but to me the chair meant death, as sure as if it were a real electric chair. It meant that I'd never get better.

Rachel walked with me to the top of the stairs. I took a step down.

"Aren't you going to ride down?" she asked, pointing at the black chair.

I shook my head. I couldn't ride the chair down now. At that moment, I was done thinking about death.

I took each step slowly, hanging on to the railing. Rachel followed me. I had to stop three times on the way down to catch my breath and rest. At each stop I gasped for air, feeling dizzy and tired. I probably looked more like I was eighty years old than fourteen.

I felt my heart pound in my chest, straining to keep up. Rachel reached out to take my arm, but I nudged her away.

The third time I stopped, Mom came looking for me. She put her hands on her hips. "Amelia, what are you thinking? We have to hurry. You should have taken the chair down."

But I was almost to the bottom. Mom watched, holding her breath. I knew she wanted to pick me up and carry me the rest of the way, all seventy-three pounds of me. Kyle already weighed fifty-eight pounds, and he was just seven years old.

Mom shook her head. "Why are you doing this?"

But behind her, Aunt Sophie was nodding, as if she understood. It wasn't about hurrying. It wasn't about pride, either, as Mom probably thought. I'd taken the chair hundreds of times in front of other people. I wasn't ashamed that I needed to use it.

I wanted to walk down the stairs because I wanted to feel my worn-out heart before they tore it out of me. This would be the last time I'd ever walk down these steps with this heart.

Rachel promised me a new life with endless possibilities. I wanted that new heart and the new life that came with it. But first I had to leave the old one behind.

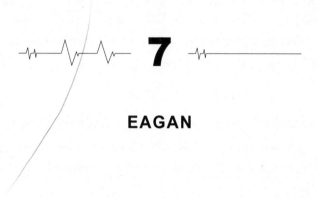

7

EAGAN

The only prayer I can think of has to do with the Lord being a shepherd and dwelling in His house forever. I'd settle for a shack or hut, but all I see is gray.

Enough of this. I have to find a way back to my life. I start walking and even though I'm sure I don't have a body, I *feel* my feet moving. When I look down, there they are. Skaters have ugly feet. Mine are no exception. They're the same as always: the blisters on my left heel, the corn at the side of my right foot. Only the blisters don't hurt at all. And something else: my feet are as gray as the fog. In fact, all of me is gray, even the skating dress I'm wearing. I blend into the fog like a single tree in a forest.

I walk through the thick fog that seems to stretch on indefinitely. I wonder how far it goes. I don't get tired, so I keep walking. The whole time, I feel the presence of others, but I don't see anyone. Finally I get bored of the grayness.

"Hey!" I call out. I hear background noise, as though it's coming from far away, but it never gets any louder no matter which direction I turn. I half expect someone to jump out and scare me, to shout, "Gotcha!" and then I'll wake up.

Mom had a habit of sneaking up on me. But she's not background noise. She's more like white noise, a radio station that isn't quite tuned into a signal. Just as I think this, another memory flashes in front of me.

On my sixth birthday, Mom baked a double-layer chocolate cake. I licked the bowl after she stuck the cake in the oven, and I watched through the glass doors as it rose in two perfect circles.

Then Mom decorated the cake with white frosting and drew six balloons in my favorite color, purple. In purple letters she wrote "Happy Birthday, Eagan!" across the top. The cake announced to the whole world that I was the birthday girl and I was special.

I sat on the steps by the back door, waiting for Dad to get home from work so we could start the party. I had on my navy jumper and the black shiny shoes Grandpa and Grandma had sent me from Florida where they were vacationing.

Dad finally arrived, and I spent the next half hour picking at my plate of Swiss steak and mashed potatoes. I only had eyes for that cake. Then Dad asked me what I wanted for my birthday.

"I want a sister," I said. A classmate had shown pictures of her new baby sister during show-and-tell, and I wanted one too.

Dad bent down and kissed me on the forehead.

"Now that's quite a birthday wish."

But Mom's lips pinched up real tight and her voice sounded

high, like all the air had gone out of it. "Eagan, you don't wish for things like that."

"Cheryl, she didn't mean anything."

Mom was cutting my cake and shoving it onto plates. Chocolate crumbs flew across the blue and white checkered tablecloth. I hadn't even blown out the candles yet. "Richard, don't encourage her. You always take her side."

Mom looked down at me. Her eyes were angry. "We're not having any more children, so don't *ever* say that again."

Dad stood up. "I won't let you do this to her, Cheryl. She's not to blame."

"Are you saying that I am?"

"No, of course not."

I wished I could take back my birthday wish. I didn't know it would make Mom so upset.

Mom was making a mess of things. She held the knife in the air and twirled it around then plunged it down into the center of the cake.

"Eagan, go to your room. Your father and I are having a discussion."

That's what she always said when they were going to yell at each other.

But Dad stood up. "How can you do this? How can you ruin a little girl's birthday?"

"Don't contradict me. I told her to go to her room."

I looked at my cake one last time before I went to my room. The layers of chocolate with creamy white in between. The six pink candles centered in each purple balloon. I hadn't even had a bite of it. I felt like a prisoner sent to jail.

From my room I heard them yelling. I heard Mom crying. I heard Dad's low voice, hissing as he tried not to yell. Then I fell asleep on my bed, above the covers, waiting for them to come and get me and finish the party.

The next morning, Dad nudged me awake. He sat on the edge of my bed with two presents in his hands. "Happy birthday, sweetheart."

Mom stood at the door holding a cup of coffee, smiling as though nothing had happened the night before.

I ripped off the paper and ribbon. I got a new sweater and skirt and an Olympic Skater Barbie. I wound up my Barbie and watched her spin around in her blue and purple outfit, her perfect hair flipping up and down. "Thanks, Mommy and Daddy."

"You're welcome, sweetheart. I'm off to work now." Dad kissed me on the cheek and left.

"Time for you to get ready for school," Mom said. "Why don't you wear your new outfit?" Her voice was light and happy, not at all mad, as if the mommy from last night was just a bad dream.

I got dressed and put my new Barbie in my bag for show-and-tell. She had long hair pulled back in a ponytail like mine. Mom never bought me the Princess Barbie. I had Astronaut Barbie and Gymnast Barbie, and a Barbie doll dressed in a little gray suit with a miniature cell phone and a briefcase, driving a sporty convertible.

I gathered up the crumpled wrapping paper from my presents and went downstairs to throw it away. When I opened the lid of the garbage can, there, on top of the garbage, was my cake. The double-layer chocolate with white frosting and purple balloons drawn on top stared up at me. A couple of unlit candles still stuck to the balloons.

How could Mom throw away my cake? Was I that bad?

My name trailed down the sides of the plastic garbage bag in runny purple frosting. I'd had my heart so set on eating the chocolate layers that it tore me up inside to see it mixed up with the potato peelings and coffee grounds. I felt like that cake, all smashed up and forgotten.

I reached down and grabbed a chunk of chocolate cake and stuck it in my mouth, smearing purple frosting on my new sweater. The cake was delicious. I jammed another large hunk of cake into my mouth, making more of a mess on my face and clothes. I ate more, smashing swirls of chocolate and white and purple into my mouth.

Mom came into the kitchen then. She folded her arms and stared at me, covered in chocolate crumbs and purple and white frosting, with smears on my face and new sweater. I waited for the outburst, the screaming, the spanking. But her face was calm, not like the face of the mom from last night. All she said was, "Go change your clothes, Eagan. Those are dirty." She didn't even say it in an angry way. She said it like she was saying to wash my hands or get my coat on, like it was no big deal.

Last night's mom had a harsh voice and looked at me with angry eyes. Today's mom had kind eyes and a soft voice.

That afternoon, when I got home from school, there was another cake on the table: a store-bought cake, bigger and fancier than the one she'd thrown away. This cake had a figure skater drawn on top and pink trim around the top and sides. My name was written in fancy letters, and the candles were set in little yellow candleholders.

Mom put her arm on my shoulder when I saw the cake. "Isn't it beautiful?" she said with a sigh. Next to the cake were two tickets for the ice show where I could see Michelle Kwan in person.

We sang "Happy Birthday" at dinner, and I blew out the candles. Mom smiled at me and opened a pint of chocolate swirl ice cream to put on top of the cake.

"I want an extra big piece," Dad said as he winked at Mom, and I knew that everything was right again.

That cake tasted good. But the cake in the garbage tasted better. It was the best cake I ever ate.

 **8**

Amelia

Mom missed the exit to the hospital. She never misses the exit. Never, ever. But that day, the day we were going to get my new heart, she did.

"Oh, no!" Mom banged her hand on the steering wheel when she realized what she'd done. "I can't believe I missed it."

"There's another exit half a mile up," I said, pointing toward the sign above us. "You can just get off there."

Mom shook her head. "I'll have to turn around and go back to that exit. That's the only way I know how to get there."

She clutched the steering wheel. The veins in her hand stuck out like ridges on a potato chip. It was as if a rubber band was holding her together and it was ready to snap.

I wasn't much better. My hands were clammy, and I felt like puking even though I hadn't eaten all day. How would I feel with someone else's heart beating inside me? I wasn't sure I'd still be me.

And what if I died? I *could* die. There would be such a hole in our family. Poor Kyle, his cards forever lying in a mess on my bedroom floor. Poor Mom and Dad, having to plan a funeral when they were so full of hope that this would work.

Poor me. Never growing up, stuck forever at the age of fourteen. I'd be dead. I was too young to be dead.

Another person was already dead. Wasn't that enough to balance out the universe? I hoped God wouldn't take me too. I hoped this other person's heart would work in me. But what if it didn't?

I started shaking. My whole body rattled. I held on to the doorknob but I couldn't stop. What if they couldn't do the transplant now because we were late?

"Mom!" I grabbed her arm. She had driven up to the next exit and stopped at a red light. "Something's wrong with me. I can't stop shaking."

Mom reached over and grabbed my wrist. "It's okay. You're nervous, honey. But this is going to work. Believe me, Amelia. This is your chance for a normal life. You are going to grow up and go to college and get married and have children of your own. You are going to live. We just have to get through this. You understand?"

I nodded. If Mom wanted me to live this bad, then I was going to live. My body seemed to listen to her and calmed down. Now only my hands shook.

Mom drove back to the last exit, turned right, and hit only green lights the rest of the way. "Okay now," Mom said as each light flicked green in front of her, as if she'd made them turn. She sat up in her seat and pressed down on the pedal, speeding ten miles over the limit. We were on a mission.

She pulled the car up in front of the revolving front door of the hospital.

"Aren't you going to the parking ramp?" I asked, suddenly wishing I had more time.

Mom turned off the car and grabbed her purse. "We'll let the valet take the car." She got out and gave her key to the man in a white shirt and black tie.

I opened the car door and inhaled a breath of autumn air. In spite of the sun, the air held a crisp chill, a reminder that winter wasn't far away, but summer wasn't far behind. I winced at the usual pain of breathing deeply. We were here, but now I wasn't in any rush to get inside. The glass doors loomed in front of me. Doors I might never come out of again.

No one had asked me if I wanted this. Not Mom or Dad or Dr. Michael. It was just the next step in my treatment, another chance at life. Sure, I'd gone through a battery of tests and met with the transplant coordinator. Even someone from the psych department. I'd been evaluated to make sure I was a good candidate. But nobody ever really asked if this was what I wanted. And even if they'd asked, I would have said, "Yes, I want a heart. I want to live." Because I knew that half of all patients waiting for a heart don't get one.

But what if I changed my mind now? How much longer could I live without a transplant? If I died today, I'd lose that time. Time to be with my family. Time to say good-bye. I never said good-bye to Kyle. How could I let them rip out my heart and put in a different one when I hadn't said good-bye to my little brother?

I took small steps toward the door. Mom was behind me. I stopped once to catch my breath and saw Mom breathing extra hard, as if she was taking up the slack, breathing for both of us.

"Wait here," Mom said, and she hurried inside.

A flock of geese honked overhead as they flew in their V formation. Dad told me that when a sick goose can't keep up, two geese drop out of formation and stay with it until it dies or is able to fly again. Then if and when it's healthy, they fly together to find another flock to latch on to.

Mom promised that she or Dad would stay at the hospital around the clock. Even though they wouldn't be able to sleep in my room, they'd be close by. And tucked inside my suitcase was my baby blanket, a yellow and white blanket with a teddy bear in pajamas embroidered on the front that Aunt Sophie had made for me when I was born. The blanket had a rip in one corner and frayed edges, but I'd had it with me during every hospital stay.

Mom came back with a nurse pushing a wheelchair. I sat down on the gray seat, hugged my suitcase close like a shield, and took one last look at the sky. I waved at the geese and wished them well.

9

EAGAN

These aren't just memories. I'm actually there, living it all over again. I can smell the pipe tobacco on Dad's shirt. It makes me feel warm inside. I can feel the soft carpet beneath my toes and the cold linoleum that makes my feet freeze. I can hear the creak of the stairs and the ticking of the clock on the mantel.

But the one thing I can't do is change anything. No matter how hard I try, it plays out as it did before. I say the same words, have the same reactions, do the same things that I did before. It's like being stuck in a rerun.

If I can't get back to my life, I might as well revisit it the only way I'm able to now. Anything is better than this dismal grayness. I search my heart for some warm memories. When they wash over me, the fog begins to lighten.

The first time I tried on a pair of skates I was hooked. It was a pair of white figure skates with pink laces that I got for

Christmas when I was three years old. I tried them out on the pond behind our house that same day. Dad had to drag me off the ice when my cheeks turned as pink as my laces and my nose was nearly frozen. I cried because I didn't want to stop skating.

Mom had been at church. When she got back, she was furious.

"What's the matter with you, Richard? Those aren't pond skates. She'll ruin them out there."

"Sorry, Cheryl. I didn't know."

"That's the problem. You don't know anything about skating. She'll get proper training with the learn-to-skate program at the local rink. The *indoor* rink."

"I'm sorry, Mommy," I cried, because she was mad. "Please don't take away my skates."

Mom bent down and gave me a hug. "I'm not mad at you, Eagan. I'm glad you love skating. And I won't take them away. Not ever. Okay?"

"Okay," I whimpered.

"These are special skates for indoors only," she explained. "We'll get you a different pair of skates for the pond. But once you skate on indoor ice, I promise you won't want to skate on the pond again."

She was partly right. Pond ice was uneven and unpredictable. Even on indoor ice, one degree could change the conditions of the rink. It could change how your skates gripped the ice or how you landed your jumps.

But nothing beat skating on a pond, eating snowflakes on your tongue as you glided across the ice with your dad holding your hand, watching as a border of fresh snow decorated the pine trees. Dad made sure the ice was kept smooth and clean, and he even put two lawn chairs on the edge so we could take breaks.

One day, Dad wasn't home from work, and I was skating alone on the pond. It was snowing lightly, but not enough to clog the rink with snow. I looked up to see Mom across from me on the ice, skating toward me. I wasn't supposed to skate outdoors alone. I thought I was in trouble. Plus, I'd never seen Mom on the ice before. I didn't even know she owned a pair of skates. I searched her face for signs of anger but saw something else. I wasn't sure what.

Mom's dark hair was sprinkled with falling snowflakes. She looked so pretty. She didn't even have a coat on, just a down vest over a turtleneck shirt and blue spandex pants. She lifted her foot and glided on one skate toward me. Then she turned at the last minute, put her arms in a circle, and arched her back; her hands went up and her head relaxed back and she spun around on one skate, going faster as she brought the circle of arms closer to her body.

She looked as graceful as Tara Lipinski. Finally she slowed down, straightened up, and pulled out of the spin.

I was breathless. "I didn't know you could skate like that."

She huffed out breaths of cold air. Her lips parted into a smile. "I used to be pretty good at one time." She skated around me.

"Why don't you skate anymore?"

Mom crinkled her nose. "That's a good question. I guess I'm just too busy."

"Skate with me, Mommy," I begged. "Please?"

She bent down and took my hands. I felt her warm breath on my face. "Anything for you, Eagan."

She led me backward across the ice, making figure eights

and going in circles until I was dizzy. We skated a long time, until my nose started running. Then we went inside and had hot chocolate.

That was the only time I remember seeing Mom skate. It was one magical moment between the two of us.

As I relive it now, I realize it's my favorite skating moment. I saw a side of Mom that she didn't often show. But I never asked her about her skating dreams. I never found out how far she'd gone in her own skating career. The fog that surrounds me is lifting. Maybe this memory has something to do with that.

It occurs to me that there's a reason I'm here. But what is it? Maybe it's to wander around the dark edges of my life. Or to celebrate the life I had. If I'm dead, then I know that there's one thing that continues in the afterlife: frustration.

10

Amelia

I woke up with a dry mouth, like I'd spent a week in the desert without water. I tried to speak. No sound came out. There was something in my throat; a tube connected to a machine snaked down inside me.

I wanted to grab the tube, but my arms didn't move. I turned my head. The tube turned too. My arms felt heavy, as if they were tied down.

A nurse in a blue smock was checking a beeping machine right next to me. I wanted her to look at me. I willed her to look at me.

She didn't turn. I tried again to move my arms. So heavy. My throat was uncomfortable. Tears ran down my face, past my nose, and into the corners of my mouth.

The ventilator had a strong smell, like antiseptic air. No matter what I'd read beforehand, I wasn't prepared for the tube down my throat or my inability to swallow. My stomach felt queasy. Where were Mom and Dad?

I blinked in the bright light above me, trying to adjust my

eyes. Was the operation over? What was happening? Why did I feel so odd? I tried to focus on the back of the nurse's smock, but the blue blended into the walls and she turned fuzzy.

There was something strange about me. Something besides all the tubes and wires that snaked from my body as if from an overused outlet.

I screamed but nothing came out. I was trapped in a nightmare. Yes, that's what was happening. I had to go back to sleep so I could wake up in my own bed. That was easy enough. My eyes were so heavy. I wasn't even surprised when the nurse turned into a horse, Dusty, the same mare I'd ridden before in my dream.

I was on top of the horse, riding higher and faster than I'd ever thought possible. The horse came to a white fence and jumped over, turning in the air as he jumped. We hit the frozen ground. I hung on, dizzy and afraid that I'd fall and puke at the same time. I bumped my head on the horse's mane. Pain shot through me but I didn't let go. I clutched his ears and mane, holding on for dear life. It felt as if my weak heart would give out before my arms did, and I'd pass out or let go if the horse ran much longer. If I fell, I was sure I would be trampled by his hooves as he ran past.

Then suddenly everything felt calm. I was still on top of the horse, still galloping at full speed through a grassy pasture, but now a surge of strength seemed to fill me from inside out. I felt free. I took a deep breath, a wonderful pain-free breath of fresh air. The ground streaked by, but I wasn't scared anymore. The horse felt secure beneath me, and my body fell into his rhythm.

I was one with this horse now, riding fast and free. A fluid motion of inner strength and balance traveled from the horse's back and neck up into me, filling me with a powerful energy. We were fearless.

Energy. Power. Freedom. I could breathe, I could shout. I felt so alive.

Was I dead? Was this how death felt? More alive than when I *was* alive?

"Go, Dusty," I yelled, and I put my hands in the air because I knew that now I didn't have to hold on. I wouldn't fall.

The horse turned his head in midstride, and his voice drifted back on the prairie wind. "My name isn't Dusty. Call me Dynamo." The voice seemed to come from both the horse and from inside me. It sounded higher than my voice.

"Dynamo." I repeated the name because I wanted to remember it. "Dynamo, Dynamo, Dynamo."

Then I opened my eyes again. The tube was gone, and those were the first words that came out of my mouth.

11

EAGAN

Now that the fog isn't so dense, I can see farther out. An ocean of gray stretches as far as I can see. It seems the longer I'm here, the more I feel part of the fog, as though I'm made out of gray nothingness.

The fog lifted when I relived the good memories. So I decide to concentrate on those. I've got to get out of this awful place. I have to be more than nothing. More than air. More than grayness.

I go back to a few months ago, before everything changed.

"Don't put it on too thick," Grandpa warned for the fourth time.

"I'm not, old man. I'm doing it just right."

"Our first joint project may be our last, young lady."

I used a tiny brush to apply a thin layer of varnish to the rocking chair. Grandpa had done the structural work; his hands seemed to know what to do on their own. I sanded the wood, brushed it with steel wool, and applied a tung oil and resin finish, working in his open garage to avoid the fumes.

"You can dish it out, Grandpa, but you can't take it."

He sat on an overturned trash can wearing a checkered flannel shirt that had white paint stains across the sleeves. He'd rolled up the sleeves as the afternoon sun warmed the garage. Every so often he picked up a broom and pushed out the red and gold leaves that blew in close to the chair. The paper-thin skin of his arms jiggled as he swept. His bifocals rested at the end of a stubby nose but he never pushed them up.

"You shouldn't be such a smart aleck. When I'm teaching you how to do something, you should listen to me."

"I am listening. But you act like it's torture for you to watch me do this. You want to do it yourself?"

He shook his head. "You're doing fine. Just keep it consistent."

"I'll keep it consistent, all right."

"And don't talk back." Grandpa tried not to smile but I saw one brewing beneath his white mustache. He liked that I sassed him back, but he'd never admit it.

Grandpa stuck out a finger. "Look. It's dripping down the side." He reached for the brush, but pulled back his hand. It was killing him to watch someone else struggle at what came so easily for him.

"Got it." I caught the drip with the edge of the brush.

Grandpa grunted. The brush was like a magnet drawing him toward it.

"I'm going to make you go in the house if you don't stop," I warned him.

He grabbed the broom and turned away from me, mumbling something about kids.

"I heard that," I said. Grandpa didn't reply. He pushed the broom across an oil stain in the center of the garage and allowed me to work. I glanced over at him, at his bent-over body. He looked so frail.

This chair had required such intricate work. My back hurt from bending over while I brushed on the varnish. How had Grandpa managed?

"I'm not sure Mom is the rocking type," I said as I dipped the brush into the old margarine tub now filled with golden liquid.

Grandpa placed the broom between two shovels. "A good rocker relaxes a person. Believe me, I know what I'm talking about." When he wasn't tinkering around in his basement or garage, Grandpa spent his evenings on his front porch rocking chair.

"Mom sure needs relaxing. She's the most uptight person I know."

"It isn't easy working and raising a teenager. Not in today's world."

"She works part-time, Grandpa. How hard can showing houses be? I think she just enjoys ripping apart other people's houses, telling them what they need to do to make them showable."

"So she's high-strung. Your father knew that when he married her. But she's a good woman."

It bothered me that Grandpa always defended her. I stopped to rest my arm. "I wonder where she'll put it."

"In the spare bedroom," Grandpa said without hesitation.

"Why would she put the chair there? We don't even use that room."

"Grandpa wisdom," he said. That's what Grandpa always said when he didn't want to explain his reasoning.

Did Grandpa mention the spare bedroom because he didn't think Mom would want a handmade rocking chair in her living room? She *was* that picky about her furniture.

"You realize that Mom replaces the furniture in our house every three years," I warned him. "All this work might end up at the Goodwill."

"Maybe she'll pass the chair on to you when she doesn't need it any longer," Grandpa said.

"I hope so. This chair is great." I stood back to admire my work.

Grandpa had selected Oregon black walnut, which he had specially shipped to Milwaukee. He'd carved the letter *L* for Lindeman, our last name, into the top and had taken extra care to make sure the grain followed the curves of the chair. Then he'd made me sand it. Five times! Each time I had to use finer and finer sandpaper.

Grandpa whistled. "Look at that sheen. See why I had you sand it five times?"

"Yeah, so my arm would fall off." I had to admit I'd never seen a more beautiful rocking chair.

But something nagged at me. Rockers didn't fit Mom's taste in furniture. Last summer she'd bought a white Italian leather sofa for the living room. Even though our house was old, it had been remodeled so that the inside looked brand new.

I sighed and sat the brush on the edge of the margarine tub. My fingertips stuck to each other. After this coat dried, I had to apply another one. I was hot and tired. The ends of my ponytail stuck to the back of my sweaty neck. Would Mom even appreciate all our work? I doubted it. As Grandpa said, this chair might end up in the spare bedroom where nobody would see it.

"If Dad knew that Mom was like that, why did he marry her? She's so high maintenance."

Grandpa shrugged. "Same reason he's still married to her. She has a lot of good qualities: she's determined, loyal, hard-working."

"Sounds like a dog."

"Sounds kind of like you."

"Don't ever say that. Don't compare me to *her*."

"I know you two butt heads. That's part of you growing up. But don't be so quick to judge. Wait until you know her better."

"I'm her daughter. How much better can I know her?"

"There's knowing her now and knowing her ten years from now."

I frowned. "What does that mean?"

"You don't know everything yet."

"Like what?"

Grandpa shook his head. "You have to clean out that brush before it dries."

"No, really. What don't I know?"

"It's not my place. Time to call it a day."

Grandpa wouldn't budge. I put the lid on the margarine tub and stuck the brush in a can of turpentine.

Maybe I didn't know everything about Mom, but I knew her well enough. And I knew one thing Grandpa didn't know: that his idea to make a homemade rocking chair for her was a waste of time. She wouldn't like it. Nothing Grandpa thought he knew could convince me otherwise.

12

Amelia

I woke up in a fog of lights and buzzing machines. So strange. Something nagged at me. What had I forgotten? The last few days were like a groggy movie in my brain. I struggled to find the words when the breathing tube came out. My mouth was too dry to talk.

Mom sat in a chair next to me reading a celebrity gossip magazine. A surgical mask covered her mouth and nose; her blond hair was crushed up against her neck. She had on a green gown over her brown-striped sweater. That same sweater she always wore when I was in the hospital. Did she feel the same way about her sweater as I felt about my baby blanket?

"You're awake, sweetheart," she said when she saw me turn my head.

I'd been awake on and off; they'd even had me up to use the bathroom. Days and nights blurred into the fluorescent light above my bed. Machines beeped and blue-gowned figures floated in and out of my room. I remembered talking to Mom and Dad and maybe Aunt Sophie. It was hard to tell who was behind the masks.

"What day is it?" I squeaked out, then coughed.

"Thursday, six a.m. Two days since your transplant."

"I feel different."

Mom's eyes widened. "Does something hurt?"

"No," I said quickly. "I just feel kind of strange. My heart sounds different." Where was the swishing sound, the irregular rhythm I'd grown used to hearing every day? What was that feeling beneath the painkillers, that someone had taken the stack of books off my chest and replaced it with a feather?

And the other feeling, that this heart was sitting in a space that wasn't quite right, not the exact size and shape as it was used to. As if there was too much room. I thought of Kyle's Legos, when he pushed two bricks together that didn't really fit. It was unsettling.

Mom's eyes relaxed. She reached over and pushed my long bangs off my forehead. She was wearing surgical gloves, and I flinched at the plastic feel of her touch. "You have a healthy heart inside you now, one that can keep up with your body."

"Yeah, maybe that's it."

I twisted my head toward the heart monitor, a miniature screen with wavy lines that beeped loudly whenever one of my patches came loose. Numbers flashed out my heart rate, numbers that went up and down depending on whether a nurse was poking me with a needle or messing with the chest tubes.

An IV line in my wrist provided easy access to check my blood levels. Another IV line in my arm was used to give medication. Tubes from my chest poked out through the blanket and attached to a suction device that made a *whoosh* sound as it sucked fluid away from my heart.

Eight years of being sick had made me a deep thinker. I wasn't like other fourteen-year-olds. And I couldn't help but think about the time during the operation when there was nothing in my chest: when they removed my heart, and before they put the other heart in. When I was connected to the heart and lung machine. When I was technically dead. I wondered if that was the weird feeling I'd had.

But I wasn't dead now. My fingertips were pink. I didn't remember them ever being so pink. My face felt flushed. I'd been shutting down before, when my fingers grew tight with fluid, when my legs felt like fire hoses, when I walked like an eighty-year-old woman instead of a teenage girl. Now that was gone, along with my old heart. I felt like a flower blossoming in the spring air, coming back to life.

"They have a surprise for you today," Mom said, and her eyes sparkled.

She'd said the same thing yesterday, and they'd taken out one of the chest tubes, and the catheter from my neck. I was glad to get rid of the tube, but the pain of having it removed was so bad I had to have extra pain medication. Which machine could they unhook from me today? I hated the little patches on my chest. They stuck to my skin and made round red blotches that itched. But I knew they wouldn't be removing the heart monitor anytime soon. And I needed the IV for pain medication. They never took out the IVs until right before a person went home. That seemed like a long time from now.

Maybe they'd take out another chest tube. Or maybe the surprise was Kyle. He hadn't been up to see me yet. Was Mom's big surprise a visit from my little brother? Or a visit from Rachel?

Cards and flowers lined the window ledge. Kyle had

painted a picture of a hospital bed with a stick figure that was supposed to be me. "Come home soon, Meely" was written underneath in neon green paint. A stuffed pony sat on the cart next to my bed.

"Who sent the horse?" I asked, wondering if that was the surprise.

"Grandma. She's called every day from Kansas City. Maybe you'll be awake to talk to her today."

I coughed, expecting the familiar pain that usually came with my coughs. I held the heart pillow to my chest, the one the transplant team had given me so it wouldn't hurt as much when I coughed. My stitches hurt, but my new heart didn't. This new heart that wasn't really mine. A present from someone I didn't know. A present that didn't fit quite right.

I couldn't help but think about that someone, even though the therapist who'd evaluated me before the transplant said that worrying too much about the donor could cause undue anxiety. But she didn't say how I was supposed to *not* worry. I mean, another family was planning a funeral right now while mine was celebrating.

I felt unworthy of this gift. I didn't even know how to live.

One of the tubes rubbed against my side and I shifted in the bed. Mom fussed around the mattress, trying to straighten the sheet underneath me.

I cleared my throat and coughed again before I spoke. "Did they say whose heart I have?"

Mom's hand froze on the sheet. Her voice was soft. "A teenager's."

I vaguely remembered a dream, one with a horse. The

memory of it had been knocking around in my brain for the last two days. "Do you know her name?"

"No. We don't even know if it's a girl. The information is kept private to protect the donor's family. All we know is that he or she chose to be an organ donor on his or her driver's license."

"Oh." I'd expected more information. I pictured a girl. I wondered what she looked like, what grade she was in, if she was pretty or athletic. Did she have a boyfriend who was missing her right now? Was someone crying about her even as Mom was tucking in my sheets?

"Maybe when you're better, you could write a thank-you note to the family. The hospital will forward the letter for you."

I almost laughed. This wasn't like a Christmas or birthday gift. A thank-you note for a heart? What would I say? I'll get a lot of use from your gift? Thanks for thinking of me?

"Maybe," I said. "What's the surprise?"

Mom didn't have a chance to answer. Two green figures entered my room carrying a portable treadmill.

I thought they had the wrong room. I looked at Mom, who nodded as if she'd read my mind.

Her eyes smiled at me. "Believe it or not, you're going to be walking on that today."

I shook my head. I'd only been out of bed a few times since the transplant. I had stumbled up and down the hall once. With assistance.

Could I actually exercise? My brain said no way. But this new heart felt like it wanted to move, like it needed to move. This new heart that came from a teenager, maybe a girl with lots of energy and lots of plans before her life ended.

Mom picked up the phone. "I should call your dad. He'll want to know that you're awake."

I snorted. "Yeah. Sound the alarm. Amelia is awake."

Mom put her hand over the mouthpiece. "What did you say, sweetheart?"

My cheeks burned. "Nothing," I said. How could I talk to Mom that way after all she'd done for me? Mom, who always knew just what to say to make me feel better, whose hands held magic in them when she rubbed my back and made me feel instant relief.

But resentment filled my brain. Sharp words were ready to roll out of my mouth at any moment. They coated my tongue and I turned my head away before they escaped.

What was wrong with me? Why did I feel this way? As Mom talked on the phone, I couldn't help myself. I waited until she turned the other way. Then I reached over to the sheets she'd just tucked in and quietly pulled them back out.

13

EAGAN

"Can anyone hear me?" I scream. There's nothing except a distant noise that sounds like faraway voices. I push through the layers of fog, which isn't hard because they're as light as wisps of air. In front of the fog is a grassy hill, but it's across a deep abyss. There are people there. I can't see their faces, but I can tell that they're old and young, male and female. Some have beards and are dressed in gowns. Some wear uniforms. Others are in suits and dresses. They're all the same race through the fog: gray.

"Hey," I call, but they're too far away to hear me. Their voices are the ones I've been hearing. No words, just indistinct human sounds.

I want to cry or punch someone. There *has* to be a way out of here. I concentrate on finding the best moment of my life. And I know just where to start.

I met Scott my first week at Harding High. The halls were empty except for a few stragglers rushing to class as I struggled to open my locker. My math homework was locked inside.

"Damn." I pounded my hand against the metal.

"Hey, soph," a voice called over my shoulder. "Move aside."

My head barely came up to the broad shoulders resting beneath a red letter jacket. An assortment of pins and patches ran down both sleeves. The guy wearing the jacket had blue eyes and short black hair. Kelly had told me to avoid upperclass guys, but he positioned himself in front of my locker, so I had no choice.

"What's your combo?" His hand rested on my lock.

"Like I'd tell *you*?"

"Fine, but you won't get this thing open. This was my locker last year. It has a catch."

"What catch?" I eyed him suspiciously.

"Tell me your combo and I'll show you." He grinned at me, showing off a dimple in his left cheek.

"Can't you just tell me?"

"It's complicated."

"It's a locker. How complicated can it be?"

"A soph with an attitude. I like it. But if you don't want my help, I guess you can figure it out on your own. It only took me two months to master."

He turned to leave.

"Wait." I hesitated. I doubted he'd want to steal the contents of my locker: three books, two notebooks, a mirror, and my skates so I could leave straight for practice after school.

"I won't write it down," he said, as he rested his right arm above me on the locker. A huge football-shaped patch stared down at me. He was still smiling; his dimple cut deeper into his cheek.

The hallway was empty now. I was late. I let out a short breath. "Fifteen, twenty-four, five."

He flipped the combo like a pro, then took his fist and slammed the upper left corner of the locker. The door flung open.

"Make sure to hit this spot," he said, pointing to where he'd slammed his fist. A small gray indentation marked the place. "What's your name, soph?"

"Eagan."

He shifted his books in his left arm. "Well, Eagan, do you think you can get it open yourself now?"

I shrugged, wondering the same thing myself.

"Then I'll have to stop by again tomorrow to see if you need help."

And he did. He stopped by the next day and every day after that for three weeks. He called me soph and admitted that he'd memorized my combination. That was how he managed to put a long-stemmed rose in my locker with a note asking me to homecoming.

I asked Kelly about him on our way to practice that day.

"I can't believe Scott Hadley asked you to homecoming."

"Why? I'm not exactly a freak or anything."

"It's just that I know of at least six senior girls who have a crush on him. But they say he's kind of shy outside of football."

I shook my head. "He's not shy around me."

"So, are you going with him?"

"You know how my mom feels about boyfriends. And she puts football on the bottom rung of sports, right next to boxing."

"But it's your life, remember?"

I sighed. "Supposedly."

It was common knowledge that behind every great skater was a pushy mom. All the great ones, from Peggy Fleming to Tara Lipinski, had moms who put their own lives on hold to promote their child's dream.

In Mom's defense, she tried to stay out of the rink other than the one practice a week. Other moms were there every day. Some read or worked while their kids practiced. Others stared at their kids as though they were analyzing every movement.

But there was always pressure. It just wasn't obvious. Mom worked part-time to help pay for the cost of my skating. We didn't have family vacations like other families did. Ours were planned around skating events.

And Mom had this subliminal way of telling me what she expected. She said that international exposure would make me a better skater. She said that Kelly would have been a better skater if she hadn't had a steady boyfriend. Sure, Kelly wasn't as serious about competing as I was. But she had a life. It didn't seem fair to have to choose.

I brought home the rose the next day and gulped down a nervous breath before facing Mom. I was barely inside the door when Mom snapped, "Who in the world gave you that?"

"Scott Hadley. He asked me to homecoming."

Mom opened the cupboard. She used two hands to lift down her white vase. Her voice drifted back. "Do I know him?"

"I doubt it. He's a senior."

She turned around. "Then let him go with a senior girl."

"Mom, lots of sophomores are going with seniors."

"You have practice on Saturday mornings."

"I can go to practice and still have all afternoon to get ready."

Mom sat the vase on the counter. "Eagan, I don't want . . ."

"What's the big deal? It's just a dance."

"I'm sure that's what all the girls at Planned Parenthood will be saying six weeks from now."

I clutched at the rose as a thorn worked its way into my palm. "Do you honestly think I'd have sex with him? It's our first date!"

She didn't say anything.

"Mom, if you expect me to be a top skater, you have to let me have fun once in a while too."

Mom's eyes narrowed. "Do you have any idea how much we pay every month for this sport? You should thank us for doing this for you, for giving you a focus for your life."

"It's not a focus. It's my whole *life*."

"Don't exaggerate, Eagan."

"I'm not. Every day of the week I get up at a quarter to six, eat breakfast, and head to the rink. Then at eight I run off to school until three o'clock, then I run back to the rink and stay there till six. Oh, and I also have ballet lessons and off-ice conditioning twice a week. And of course I have to fit home-work in somewhere. I dedicate so much of myself to skating and I love it, but I want more out of life before I die."

"You know I don't like you to talk like that. You're only sixteen years old."

That was her hang-up, not mine. "Okay. I want to have something besides skating competitions to remember high school."

"You'll have a whole lifetime of memories." She turned away from me, picked up a dishcloth, and started wiping around the sink. "Besides, if you qualify for international competition, we'll need the money for a new skating outfit instead of a homecoming dress."

"Kelly is going to lend me her dress from last year. I need this, Mom. I need to have fun. Otherwise, I'm going to get burned out and I'll hate skating. I swear I'll hate it."

Mom spun around. Her voice quivered. "So if you don't go to this dance, you'll hate skating? Fine. Quit."

"I don't want to quit. I want to go to homecoming."

"I suppose next you'll hate me."

"I never said I'd hate you."

"It's the same thing."

"No, it's not the same," I said. "Whether I skate or not doesn't change how I feel about you." As I said the words, I realized they were true for me, but probably not for Mom.

"But it's all that matters to *you*," I said. "You only care about what level I'm competing at or whether I make it to Nationals or not. You don't care if I have any friends. You don't care if I have a life. You're such a—"

Mom reached over and slapped me hard on the cheek. She looked shocked, as if she couldn't believe what her hand had just done. Tears sprang from the stinging heat of her slap, but I defiantly blinked them back.

"Eagan," Mom began. I threw the rose on the kitchen floor and ran to my room.

An hour later, Mom opened my door. She didn't knock or anything; she just came in. Her eyes darted around the room. She probably wanted to say something about the clothes on the floor or the layer of dust on my dresser. She held a piece of paper in one hand and the white vase in the other, the rose sticking out the top.

"Can we talk?"

I just stared at the computer monitor in front of me.

"I lost it this afternoon." She paused. "I'm not very good at apologizing. So I wrote you something."

Finally I looked at her. "What?"

Mom handed me a paper folded in half. It was a letter that started with "Dear Eagan." I knew Mom wrote long letters to her sister who lived in Portland. But a letter to me? I stared at the paper. It reminded me of the admit slips we carried to class when we'd been absent. "Is this your excuse for slapping me?"

Mom's cheek twitched. "No, of course not. I shouldn't have lost my temper. But that wasn't entirely my fault, Eagan. You push me to my limit every time we argue."

"Right. My whole life is *you* pushing *me*."

"*If* I push, it's because you're so talented. I'm helping you achieve *your* goals. The ones *you* set. You only have a short time and then it's over." She stopped and closed her eyes. "I know you work very hard. You can go to the homecoming dance if you're back by midnight." She nodded at the paper. "Read the letter." She set the vase on my dresser and left.

I'd won this time. Not much of a victory, though. She always threw it back in my face. Just because I was a dedicated skater didn't mean that I didn't care about anything else. Who said the Olympic dream meant giving up your whole life? Who made that rule?

A lousy piece of paper. That was her apology. I crumpled it up and threw it in the wastebasket.

14

Amelia

There was something wrong with my new heart. It didn't fit the way it should. I could tell right away, the same way you can tell if a pair of jeans doesn't fit, only this was inside me and much more uncomfortable than jeans.

"It feels funny here, like my heart's not in the same spot as it used to be." I lightly touched my gown, where, underneath, a long scar ran down the middle of my chest.

Dr. Michael nodded. "Nothing is going to be exactly the same as your old heart. It's as close as we're going to get, though," he added, looking at Mom, who hovered next to me.

"Transplantation isn't a cure. You trade one set of problems, a failing heart, for another set of less severe problems, like having to take antirejection medication for the rest of your life."

He'd used the *R* word. Rejection.

"What happens if my body rejects this heart?" I asked. Mom had avoided talking about it, but I knew that Dr. Michael would tell me the truth.

"Half of all rejections happen within the first six weeks," Dr. Michael said, "and about a fourth of recipients have a rejection episode within the first year. You'll be taught which symptoms to look for. The important thing is to take your medications. We'll try to wean you off the prednisone in the first year. There are options if you have a rejection episode. We'll discuss those before you go home."

He turned to leave. "I can't promise that everything will be easy from now on, that there won't be problems. But these are problems you can live with. That's the difference." He winked at me, then left, his beeper calling him away.

I still had my hand over the spot. It wasn't just the fit of my heart, or the crooked scar that ran down almost to my stomach. It wasn't the strong meds that I was taking or the after-effects of anesthesia. I didn't know how I knew it wasn't any of those things, but I just knew. This was separate from all that. I felt different in a way I couldn't explain. *Really* different. And it freaked me out.

But Dr. Michael couldn't explain that to me, any more than I could explain how I felt different.

Mom filled my water glass from the plastic flesh-colored pitcher. "Dr. Michael said you're going to be transferred to pediatrics tomorrow."

Just yesterday I'd walked on the treadmill. My legs felt weak but I'd walked more than five minutes before stopping. And I only stopped because they told me to, not because I felt winded. I could have gone longer.

It seemed that my heart was in better shape than the rest of me. I had such strength and endurance, like an athlete. Was this how everyone felt when they had a healthy heart?

Mom was sitting in a chair with her magazine open on her

lap. Her eyes were puffy from lack of sleep. I wanted to talk about this strange feeling but was afraid she would worry or think I was exaggerating. I'd always told Mom everything. But I didn't think she'd understand this feeling that was growing inside me like a rock tumbling down a hill, gaining momentum until I felt ready to scream. I didn't understand it myself.

"How's my girl doing?" Dad said as he entered the room. He had taken the week off from work, but since I was doing so well, Mom had convinced him to go in part of the day. Dad wasn't much good in hospitals. He spent most of his time pacing the halls.

"Good," I said. I'd never tell Dad about these feelings I was experiencing. He'd say I was running a fever or something. He always expected medicine to fix everything.

"The nurse gave me this," he said, handing me a pamphlet. It was about a support group that newly transplanted patients and families were encouraged to attend.

"Do they talk about the donors?" I said. Probably not. Mom said we couldn't even know the name of my donor. Private information.

"Don't know," he said. Dad stuck his hands in his pockets and rocked back on his heels. "You'll never guess what I did today."

"What?"

"I got rid of the electric chair." He flashed a wide grin as he looked from me to Mom.

"So soon?" Mom put down her magazine.

Dad nodded. "Don't need it anymore. You saw how she did on the treadmill yesterday."

"Big deal, Dad. I walked for five minutes. Now you're

acting like I took first place at a track meet." My voice was sarcastic.

Mom and Dad stared at me. Then they looked at each other. I thought one of them would run out of the room and grab a nurse if I didn't apologize.

"I'm sorry. I'm just tired or something," I mumbled. But I felt my heart do a little skip, a small shout of joy.

I stared at my leftover food tray, the half-eaten piece of fish. How could I talk that way? When I was half-asleep yesterday, I'd heard them whispering about the cost of the transplant and the medications I'd be taking. I'd heard Dad say that even with our insurance, my medications would run three hundred dollars a month.

Dad nodded toward the door. "I met the social worker in the hall. She asked if you wanted to have a visitor, someone close to your age who's been through this. You know, to talk about any *concerns* you might have."

I looked at Mom, expecting her to answer for me.

Mom nodded. "I think it'd be a good idea."

"Okay. I'd like that," I said.

"You would?" Mom said. "That doesn't sound like you. I thought I'd have to talk you into it."

All I could say was, "I know." Because that wasn't what I'd usually say. I'd say I didn't know if I wanted to talk about it. I'd say I needed more time. I'd hide under the covers and let Mom rub my back and then I'd draw a picture of a mare in a grassy pasture. But I wouldn't want to talk to some strange kid who'd had a heart transplant.

So why did I want to talk to one now?

15

EAGAN

It's working. Ribbons of light are making the fog shrink. Instead of an ocean of gray, it's more like a huge lake.

Then I notice that some of the figures across from me look like they're kneeling in prayer. Is that what I should be doing?

We aren't churchgoers. Dad was raised Methodist, and Mom used to be Catholic. We go to church on Christmas, a nondenominational one, then skip until the next December rolls around. Yeah, we're one of those families.

But I always loved that little baby in the manger, the center of the whole world for just one night, even if we didn't pay attention to Him the rest of the year.

Just as that thought occurs to me, I hear a voice. It tells me not to be afraid to face the hard memories, to look beyond the happy ones. It tells me that now is the time to be reconciled to my soul. What does *that* mean?

"Who are you?" I call out. "Can I see you?"

"Soon," the voice says. The voice is high, like a child's.

That takes me back to another memory, one that pulls me in like a vacuum.

—⋀—

"Eagan." Mom's voice filled my open doorway. "Get down here now."

"I'm doing homework," I yelled back.

It was a small lie. I was supposed to be looking for a baby picture for a story I was writing in English. But instead I was IM'ing Scott.

> What's your middle name, Eagan?
>
> **Hermione.**
>
> Parents big Harry Potter fans?
>
> **Harry Potter wasn't even published when I was born, moron!**
>
> Sorry. R U mad at me?
>
> **No, I hate that name. Mom named me after a character in a Shakespeare play.**
>
> What play?
>
> **Don't remember, but Hermione was a beautiful queen.**
>
> So U R a queen?
>
> **Call me UR Highness. I never read the play but I looked it up online. The queen dies.**
>
> That sucks ☹
>
> **But she's restored to life at the end ☺**

"Eagan."

Gotta go.

I clicked off the screen and ran downstairs. Mom stood in the living room with her arms folded. A bowl with popcorn kernels and an empty glass lay next to my math book in front of the TV.

"What's this doing on the living room floor?" she screamed.

"I was going to pick it up."

"You know the rules."

"I'll do it in a minute. I have to get ready for practice." I turned to go back upstairs.

"Do it now."

"What difference does it make if I pick it up in five minutes?"

"It makes a difference to me. If you want to live in filth, confine it to your own bedroom."

She could be so rude sometimes. "A bowl of popcorn, an empty glass, and my book isn't filth. Why can't it wait?"

Her face had turned red and she was shouting. "Just do it now."

She called this our living room, but the curved glass coffee table looked more like a piece of art than a place to set a cup. The fluted floor lamp and the Roman shades and the Vermeer reproduction—this room didn't have a homey feel. It was more like a showroom. The TV in the corner was an afterthought, an allowance for the rest of the family.

I stood my ground. "Are you expecting company?"

"No. I don't want questions. I want you to pick this up."

"I will! Why do I have to do it this very instant?"

"Because I'm your *mother*."

"Well, *that's* a good reason. And I should wait because I'm your daughter." I shook my head as I stomped over and picked up the bowl and glass. But I couldn't let it go. "What differ-ence in the whole history of the world does this tiny mess make? And who cares, anyway? The whole world is falling apart, countries at war, disasters at every turn, and you worry about *this*."

Mom just continued to stand there, her arms folded, her mouth set in a tight line as though it might explode if she opened it.

After emptying the popcorn kernels into the garbage and putting the dishes in the dishwasher, I stomped back up to my room. I picked through my drawer where I'd stuffed the letter she'd given me after I'd cleaned out my wastebasket. I still hadn't read it.

Dear Eagan,

How did we get to this point? You're my whole life and I only want the best for you. That's why I'm hard on you. But please know that I love you more than anything else in the whole world.

Oh, *please*. I stopped reading and stuck the paper in my desk drawer, then turned back to my homework. I still needed a baby picture, but there was no way I was asking Mom to help me now. I went into her bedroom and opened her walk-in closet. The back shelf held a plastic storage box filled with extra pictures.

I flicked on the light switch and pulled the box down, nestling into a space on the floor between a shoe rack and a clothes bin, with the box between my legs. There were old pictures here, ones of Mom and Dad when they were young, looking a lot skinnier. They were holding hands, and Dad had a silly grin on his face, like he'd just said something funny. Mom's eyes were slanted toward him, and her lips were parted, like she was trying to keep from laughing. They looked, um, happy.

I set the box aside and dug farther back in the closet. I found two more boxes and a taped-up shoe box stuffed clear in the back with the word "PICS" in black marker across the top.

Who could resist a shoe box full of pictures? These photos must be really old. I slowly pulled back the dusty tape. The tape felt old, as if the box hadn't been opened in years. It felt secret. I stopped and listened for Mom's footsteps. I heard her downstairs, the sound of the mixer whirring in the kitchen.

I filed through the photos. They showed Mom with a huge belly. She was pregnant with me. Her face was round and soft, without the worry lines across her forehead that were always there now, and her hair was shoulder-length. Same color and almost as long as mine. She was sitting on a blue plaid sofa with a crocheted blanket laid across the top. I vaguely remembered that sofa and the cream-colored blanket. I remembered making forts out of it on the living room floor.

That was when our house was a home, not a showcase. When our furniture was more comfortable than the floor.

I turned over the picture and froze. Another picture of Mom with her large belly. But in this photo, a little girl was sitting next to her. A little girl in a pink pajama top about three years old with mussed-up brown hair. The blanket was laid out across both their laps as they huddled close together.

I held my breath and felt a sudden chill sweep through the closet. My hands shook as I stared at the picture, at the girl I now recognized. The little girl was me.

Then who was Mom pregnant with?

16

Amelia

"I keep waiting for it," I told Rachel.

"Waiting for what?"

"A complication. I mean, all the pamphlets talk about it, but I haven't had any yet."

Rachel pulled a lime lollipop out of her mouth. She checked out her green tongue in my makeup-sized mirror. "You don't want any, do you?"

"No. I'm just waiting for them. Sounds dumb, I know."

"That really doesn't sound like you, Amelia."

"What do you mean?"

She wiped at an invisible smudge on her thinly shaped eyebrow. Her makeup was perfect. "You sound depressed. That's not you."

"Everyone gets depressed, though. Don't they?"

She looked up from the mirror and shook back her long hair. "Not you. I've never heard you complain even when you had a crummy heart. So why now? You should be celebrating! You're going home in a few days."

"I just feel weird." I hesitated, wondering if I could put into words how I really felt, wondering if Rachel could understand when I didn't.

"You're probably just tired," she said, and put the mirror down on my bed stand. "I mean, I'm exhausted and all I've been doing is sitting."

I wanted to remind her that she'd been texting her new boyfriend every five minutes, but I didn't say anything.

She yawned to make her point. "I think it's something in the hospital air."

"Maybe." I reached for the bag of lollipops she'd brought me, but my hand fell short.

"Can you hand me a lollipop? A purple one?"

"What? You hate purple."

"I know, it's weird. And I've been craving grape juice."

Rachel handed me a purple lollipop, her eyes questioning me. "You even hate the color purple."

Why did I feel that way about purple? It seemed like an interesting color, a soothing one. I could definitely get into purple.

Rachel picked up her jacket. "I have to go to cheerleading practice. Anything you need me to bring you? Purple pj's?"

I tried to smile. It felt forced. "Bye." I waved to her back. My eyelids were heavy. I'd jogged on the treadmill today. Faster than walking. Almost like running. For ten minutes. Dad would be so excited.

I must have fallen asleep, because when I opened my eyes, two boys stood at the end of my bed. One was younger than me, maybe by two or three years. He had short, dark hair and an olive complexion, and was cracking his knuckles as he watched me. The popping noise cut through the beep of the heart monitor as he worked his way from his pinkie to his thumb. He dropped his hands down when I moved my head.

"Sorry. We didn't mean to wake you."

He flexed his fingers and shifted his weight.

The other boy nodded at me. He was older and he had the same color hair as the younger boy, but his hair touched his collar. "The nurse thought you were awake. She said a girl just left your room a minute ago."

Had Rachel left a minute ago? It seemed like hours had passed. I pushed the button on the side of the bed, raising my head up. "Hi. Who are you?"

The older boy spoke. "Ari. And this is Tomas. The social worker sent us."

Ari was kind of short and thin, but his face looked grown-up. He was older than me, probably in high school.

"She said you might want to talk."

"Talk?"

"You know. To someone who's been through this." He nodded toward the machines surrounding me.

"Oh." I studied him more closely. He didn't look like someone who'd had a heart transplant. He seemed normal, better than normal. Golden biceps grew out the sleeves of his T-shirt. "Both of you?"

"Not exactly. Tomas had a heart transplant twenty-two months ago. But he couldn't drive himself here so I volunteered."

"You're brothers," I said, even though it seemed obvious.

"Yeah," Ari said. "I didn't have the heart transplant, but I spent a lot of time at the hospital with Tomas. I kinda feel like a survivor too."

"But I can leave if you don't want me around," he quickly added.

"No. That's okay." I didn't honestly know how I felt. I wasn't prepared for their visit.

Ari moved toward a chair. "Okay if we sit?"

"Sure." My bare foot stuck out, and I pulled the end of the white sheet over it.

One of the muscles in Ari's arm flexed as he sat down. He scanned the room, his eyes pausing on the stuffed pony.

"How you feeling?"

"Okay."

He shook his head. "That's a lame question. Sorry, we're kind of new at this. You're our first postoperation visit."

"Oh." I felt a need to help them out, but I didn't know how. Ari stared at the pony a while longer. An uncomfortable silence followed. I let out a nervous cough. I remembered my baby blanket at the edge of my bed. Darn. He probably thought I was just a kid.

The boy named Tomas was thin and kind of frail-looking. "How old are you?" I asked him.

"Twelve. I was ten when I had my transplant," he answered in a soft voice.

He was small for his age. But Ari was short, too, and he had a driver's license, so he must be sixteen.

"You want to see my scar?" Tomas suddenly asked.

"What?" I was feeling embarrassed by the pony and my baby blanket, thinking they made me look younger than fourteen.

"My scar. Did you know you can tell what kind of transplant a person had by the scar? A heart scar is a straight line, a kidney scar looks like a *J*, and a liver scar looks like an upside-down *Y*." He paused. "Have you looked at your own scar?"

I pulled the covers up higher. I wasn't showing him mine.

"Tomas, lay off," Ari said. "It's obvious she isn't ready for that yet."

Ari leaned forward. "He only asked because it's one of those things you have to get out of the way, you know, and the sooner you look at it, the sooner you can get over it."

I'd caught little glimpses of it when the nurses changed the dressing, but I hadn't stood in front of a mirror yet. I knew I'd never wear a two-piece swimsuit again.

Tomas pulled up his shirt. A white line stretched down his front like a faded battle wound. I wondered what battles *he* faced before he got his new heart.

"They fade." He pulled his shirt back down. "Just so you know."

It seemed like the wrong shape for a scar. A heart transplant scar should be more unique. I was reminded of a radish Mom had made into the shape of a tulip once.

I didn't think I'd ever willingly show my scar to someone, even my parents or Kyle. Would I ever feel comfortable looking at it myself? "When did you get sick?"

"Two years ago. It happened really fast."

"One day he was playing soccer, the next he was in the hospital hooked up to a machine. Literally. It was unreal," Ari said. "He caught a virus that went to his heart."

A metal tray rattled in the hallway. It sounded like the dinner cart passing by.

Tomas turned his head toward the sound as though he recognized it. "It's weird coming up here as a regular person, not as a patient. Not that I miss it. When I reach the three-year mark, I'll only have to come in once a year."

Three years seemed so far off. I had to have a heart biopsy every week for the first four weeks. Then they'd stretch it out to once a month, then once every two months, and so on. I envied Tomas. He already only had to come in every few months.

"Do you miss playing soccer?" I'd read we couldn't do contact sports after our transplants.

He shrugged. "I ride my bike, do other stuff. It's not the same as before. But it's not that bad. It's better than . . ." His voice trailed off. He started cracking his knuckles as he spoke, then stopped when he saw me staring at his hands.

"Sorry. Bad habit."

"A gift from his donor," Ari added.

What did he say? My heart raced. I put my hand on my chest, feeling its reaction.

"What do you mean?" My voice sounded uneven.

"He never cracked his knuckles before. But his donor did."

I leaned forward. A sudden chill spread up my arms. "You know who the donor was?"

"Yeah. It's private stuff you're not supposed to know, but a nurse let it slip out that his donor died in a snowmobile accident. Then, after Tomas started acting different, I did a little research on my own."

I was shivering now. "Different how?"

"Well, Tomas was super outgoing before. Believe it or not, I was the shy one. After the heart transplant, he became quiet and shy. And more religious than before. They said it was normal but we knew different, didn't we, Tomas?"

Tomas nodded. "And I started doing this all the time." He cracked a knuckle on his right hand.

Ari lowered his voice. "Turns out Tomas's donor did that. And he was this super shy kid, an altar boy at church."

Was that the feeling I had? Was my donor's heart affecting me in ways I didn't understand? I remembered the dream with the horse, how real it had seemed. Was that connected to this feeling?

"We're not trying to freak you out or anything," Ari said. "I researched it after Tomas came home. Not everyone feels this way, but some heart transplant patients say they changed after their transplants. They took on characteristics of their donors. There's a theory that memory is not just in the brain, that other cells in the body store memory as well. Most doctors think it's the immunosuppressive drugs acting on people's minds. But we knew the personality changes in Tomas were more than just side effects from the drugs."

"How did you find your donor?" I asked.

"Why? Do you want to know who your donor was?" Tomas asked.

"Yeah. Maybe." But I definitely did. I wanted to know this girl—I was sure she was a girl. I wanted to know if she bit her nails or wrote left-handed or got sick on roller coasters. I wanted to know if she liked purple lollipops and jogging on the treadmill, if she was smart and had plans to go to law school, if she liked to read romance novels, and if she could draw as well as I could. I wanted to know everything about her. Was it normal to feel this way, to want to know? The two guys in front of me seemed normal. "Did you meet the family?"

"Yeah, with Ari's help."

Ari shrugged. "Tomas was going to write them a letter after his transplant, but I found out who they were, so we called and asked if it was okay to come visit."

"What did they say?" I was sitting up now, hanging on his every word.

Tomas smiled. "They wanted to meet me as much as I wanted to meet them."

"Was it weird meeting them?"

Tomas cracked one more knuckle before he spoke. "It was more than weird. It was like going home."

17

EAGAN

I have no real proof that I'm dead. I don't remember dying. I remember tripping, being too close to the edge, a searing pain. And then I was here.

Is this a dream? I'd never dream this place.

This can't be heaven. Where are all the choirs of angels? Where's God, the big guy with the white beard and deep voice? Where are Moses and all the other people we read about in the Bible? Where are those streets of gold? The pearly gates? It's all gray and kind of gloomy here, except for the shiny meadow on the other side. But no matter how far I walk, I never get any closer.

Then there are the people. I don't recognize anyone; they're too vague through the fog. But I feel their anxiousness for me to leave the blur of never-ending grayness, which seems to be heavy with all the problems from the world I left behind. It's almost suffocating. But I don't know how to leave, and besides, the only place I want to go is home.

Maybe this is purgatory, and I'm reliving all the bad times

so I can see what I did wrong. Or maybe there's going to be a test on my life, and that's why I'm going back over it.

And then there's that voice. The voice without a name or face. "Whoever was speaking to me, show yourself," I shout into the fog.

I miss Mom and Dad and Grandpa. I miss Scott and Kelly. I miss skating and eating peanut M&M's, especially the purple ones. I miss my life.

I let the tears flow. They drip down, big, gray droplets that match the fog. I cry and cry until there are no more tears left, until I feel empty inside. I don't think I've ever cried this hard. But a memory flashes before me, one that proves me wrong.

—————/\/—————

When I was little, I worried about Dad having a car accident on the way home from work. I'd wait at the window and watch for him. I imagined a man in uniform knocking on our door, and I'd know what had happened, and I'd be to blame because I'd thought of the accident.

Did my deepest self remember another tragedy? Was that why I always worried that something bad was going to happen? Why I tried to prepare for it in ways that most people would think was strange? Because my little-girl self had felt it?

I couldn't ask Mom or Dad about the picture. Grandpa. I'd ask him Tuesday after school. He was going to cook dinner for the two of us to celebrate finishing the rocker. I'd bought a huge red ribbon to tie around the chair; we'd keep it in his basement until Christmas.

Scott gave me a ride home in his Jeep after school on Tuesday. We talked about the upcoming dance, and the football game beforehand. Our team had beaten Brookfield the last two years in a row. We agreed that we were pretty much assured of a victory. I leaned over and gave Scott a quick kiss before I ran inside. Mom was waiting at the door.

"Why didn't you take the bus?"

"Scott said he'd give me a ride."

"I thought we agreed you didn't have time for a boy-friend."

She'd agreed. "Lay off, Mom. We're just friends."

Not exactly true, but why should I tell the truth when she'd lied to me my entire life? She said I was an only child.

"I'm not blind, Eagan."

I started to push past her.

"Eagan, Grandpa . . . had a stroke."

I stopped partway up the steps. Mom's eyes were red. She was wringing her hands. I hadn't noticed. My fingernails dug into the railing. "Is he okay?"

"A neighbor found him this afternoon on the kitchen floor. He's in the hospital. They think he may live, but you never know . . ." I turned and ran up the stairs before she could finish, slamming my bedroom door. My throat tightened and my body shook. I felt a sharp pain deep inside my chest.

Mom's footsteps sounded on the steps, but they stopped and faded back downstairs. I threw myself on my bed and wrapped my bedspread around me. I wanted to scream, but all I could do was cry into my pillow. My body shook with each sob.

How could this happen to Grandpa? Was I taking my social studies test, writing about the colonization of Africa while Grandpa lay helpless on the floor?

I got up and wiped away my tears. Even though I wasn't religious, I pleaded to God to make him better.

"Mom," I called as I hurried down the steps. "Can I go to the hospital?"

Mom hesitated. "He's in intensive care. You probably won't be allowed in."

"I don't care. I just want to go there."

"All right." Mom nodded and picked up her purse.

The car ride was silent. I was lost in thought, barely aware that Mom was beside me. Grandpa was old. I knew that. But he was so full of life. He played old tunes on his harmonica, and in the summer he filled his kitchen with smells of vinegar and watermelon as he mixed up batches of homemade watermelon pickles. He bragged about me to all his buddies. Next summer he was going to take me camping.

Had he overdone it with the rocking chair? Had all that bending and standing been too hard for him? Were the fumes from the varnish too strong?

It wasn't until we pulled into the parking lot that I thought to ask, "Where's Dad?"

"He's here. I came back to wait for you."

"Why didn't you get me out of school?"

Mom shrugged. "What could you have done?"

"Are you crazy?" I screamed. "I could have *been* there."

She put the car in park and turned toward me, her eyebrows narrowed down into almost a straight line. "Don't act so righteous with me, young lady. Your grandfather doesn't need you throwing a tantrum in the hospital. If you can't act appropriately, I'll take you home right now."

I closed my eyes tight and steadied my voice. "I'm not throwing a tantrum. I just want to see Grandpa."

Mom let out a breath and turned off the engine. "Then keep your voice down. This isn't about you, Eagan."

I stuck my hands into my jacket pockets. Tight fists squeezed out my anger onto the loose change.

I thought of the pictures I'd found, the ones she'd hidden at the back of her closet. Why were they hidden? Who were they hidden from? Mom was always so guarded, so controlling.

Today was no different. She could have gotten me out of class. She could have told me about Grandpa sooner. But instead, she hid the truth from me as long as possible. I kept my mouth shut and resisted slamming the car door.

Two elevators, both on upper floors. I pushed the button and willed the lower numbers to light up, but they stayed frozen in place. I pushed the button again and again.

"Eagan." Mom's voice held a warning.

The stairs were off to the right. "I'm walking up." I left before Mom could object.

She was waiting for me when I reached the fifth floor.

"You should have taken the elevator," she said as she walked ahead of me down the corridor.

"I wanted the exercise," I panted.

She threw back a glance. "Right."

"I did," I mumbled. Mom was at the intensive care desk talking to the nurses when I caught up. I spotted Dad in a room off to the side of the desk. He was staring out the window.

"Dad," I called. He turned around. His eyes were splotchy red. I'd never seen him cry before.

Then I saw Grandpa in that sterile bed, snoring softly. His arm had bluish marks from where he'd fallen. White tape covered his hand, where an IV pumped medicine into his transparent veins. Scruffy white stubble framed his gaunt face. His glasses sat on a metal tray, and his mouth hung halfway open.

He looked older than old. But he was alive. He was breathing.

"Grandpa," I cried. I'd thought if I always imagined the worst in life, then I'd be prepared for anything. But I wasn't prepared for this. Grandpa had almost died, and I never saw it coming.

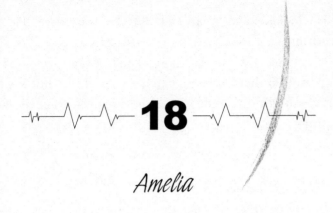

18

Amelia

It was the best I could do. I read the letter again for the fifth time.

> My name is Amelia. I'm fourteen years old. I've had a bad heart for six years, and I was put on the waiting list for a transplant three months ago. My doctor said I was lucky to get a heart when I did. I wouldn't have lived another three months.
>
> Your child's heart has given me a second chance at life. I will think of him/her every day and pray for him/her. I know this doesn't take away the loss you've suffered. Nothing could. I would like to meet you in person to thank you, if you're willing. I would like to know the

family and the person who made such a great sacrifice so that I could live.

Sincerely,
Amelia

P.S. Did your child like purple lollipops?

No last name, according to the directions on a sheet Mom had given me. Nothing beyond my first name to identify myself. I was a recipient, he or she was a donor. We were both anonymous.

Would the family write back to me? I wondered how they'd react when they read my letter, if it would make them feel any better or just be a sad reminder of what they'd lost.

I lay back as I folded up the paper and put it in an envelope. I'd been awake since five a.m. writing the letter, trying to come up with the right words. Something that would tell them how I felt. I was pretty good at writing, but how could I put in words how much their gift meant to me?

I turned off the overhead light and closed my eyes. The physical therapist would be in soon. Then more tests. How was anyone supposed to get any rest in this hospital? Especially after being moved to the pediatric ward, where screaming toddlers kept you awake half the night?

Mom complained that my room was too cold, and she constantly added more blankets to my bed, which I promptly kicked off. Before my transplant, I was cold all the time, but now it didn't bother me much. I'd been in this room for three days now, but it felt like I'd lived here forever. I'd memorized the tiles on the floor around my bed, knew the kinks of the TV (push the volume button repeatedly instead of holding it down). The hospital noises were background sounds that felt familiar now, like the furnace turning on at home. I barely noticed the beeping of the machines, and the IV felt like part of my body.

But the crying; I wasn't used to that. It sounded more than sad. It was pitiful. One night in particular it bothered me. Was it last night or the night before? The sound seemed to seep through the walls, and even the nurses acted edgy and hurried. The next morning, I'd found my own pillow wet with tears, and the ward was unusually quiet.

"Don't get too comfortable," a nurse named Sara warned as she walked in. She had a smiley face sticker stuck to the back of the stethoscope around her neck. "I need to check your vitals."

I stuck out my arm and yawned. "It's vital that I sleep."

She wrapped the blood pressure cuff around my upper arm. "You're sharp this morning."

"I didn't used to be."

"Well, you were sick a long time."

"I mean, I was never sharp that way. Ever. My donor gave me that."

"No kidding? I've heard of people developing strange tastes afterward. One lady suddenly started drinking beer, when she'd never been able to stand the taste before. Turns out her donor was a college boy who died after falling down the stairs during a frat party."

I perked up. "How did she find that out?"

Sara's eyes flicked from the blood pressure monitor to me, then back to the monitor. "Oh, I don't know if she really did.

Mrs. Lewis, the transplant coordinator, used to tell that story. It's become sort of an urban legend around here."

"But people do meet the donor families if they both want to."

Sara nodded. "Sure. I've heard that it happens. Not as often as you'd think, though."

"Maybe the lady met the college boy's family, and that's how she found out that he was a beer drinker."

"Could be."

"Unless she knew he was a beer drinker before she met the family."

"How would she know that?"

"Because her new heart told her so. She wanted to drink beer after she got his heart."

"Hmm. I'm not sure the doctors would buy that as proof."

"So, have you heard anything about *my* donor? I mean, I already know it's someone who checked the organ donor box on his or her driver's license. So I figure he or she was a little older than me, probably in high school."

Sara frowned and concentrated on squeezing the bulb that tightened the cuff around my arm. "The donor is anonymous for a reason. The family has just suffered a great loss."

I had that feeling, the one where you realize you said something embarrassing in front of your mother's friends, and you know you should apologize but you don't.

"I keep thinking my donor was a girl. It's a gut feeling I have. And I just want to know something about her, that's all. Like how she died. And," I paused, "if she was an athlete."

Sara's hand stopped midsqueeze. Her eyes widened a second. Then she resumed squeezing until my arm felt like it would burst. She slowly let out the air, her eyes focused on the flickering dial of the gauge. Finally she spoke. "What makes you think *she's* an athlete?"

"My heart feels like it wants to run, like it's used to moving a lot. Like it belonged to an athlete."

Sara's eyes darted back to the monitor. I'd seen something in her eyes, and now she was trying to act like I hadn't just caused her own blood pressure to jump. Could she know something about my donor? I doubted it, but still . . .

"Maybe you're not used to the feel of a healthy heart."

Was she trying to convince me or herself?

"No, it's more than that. Really it is."

She unfastened the cuff and hung it next to the bed. "Well, kiddo, that's something you should ask the family. Did you write a letter?"

I handed her the envelope.

Sara put the letter in her pocket. "I'll make sure Mrs. Lewis forwards this to the donor's family. There's a waiting period, though, before she can send it."

"Oh. How long?"

"I'm not sure. It might be a year."

"A year! I can't wait that long."

"They have their rules." She set the end of the stethoscope on my heart and listened. I concentrated on being still, which had never been a problem before.

Sara nodded and jotted down some numbers on my chart. "Sounds good. You'll be out of here in no time." She patted my arm. "Can I get you anything?"

I shook my head. "Sara, could I ask you something?"

"Sure, sweetie."

"If your child had died, would you want to talk to the girl who had her heart?"

She paused a moment, and yawned, stretching her arms in a circle above her. "Sorry. It's been a long day. Yes, I'd want to meet her. I'd want to put my ear to her chest, to listen to my child's heart beating, to know that in this very unique way my child was still alive to the world."

"Then tell Mrs. Lewis to send my letter now. I think they need to read it."

"You're really persistent about this. I'll see what I can do. No promises, though."

Sara put her hands back down. The sight of her standing there with her arms stretched above her head in a circle had felt familiar. I knew that sensation. But how?

19

EAGAN

She's looking straight at me. A girl. She stands out because she's not pasty gray like everything around her. Like me. She's wearing a frilly dress the same shade as the marigold bushes in Mom's garden. Her black curly hair is glittery. It reminds me of the stuff we put on our hair before competitions.

"Can you see me?" I ask.

She nods and waves like she wants to come over but needs to be invited.

Finally. Someone to talk to. My heart feels lighter. Maybe she can help me find my way back to my life.

"Hey," I say.

She doesn't need more of an invitation. She's next to me in a flash.

"I'm Eagan. What's your name?"

She's younger than I am; I'd guess she's about twelve or thirteen. She's petite like me and has the prettiest smile, the kind that melts hearts. "I don't have one." She says it with that smile still on her face.

"Why not?"

She shrugs. "No one ever gave me one."

I recognize her voice as the one I'd heard before, but she's older than she sounded. It's her voice. She sounds so happy. Maybe too happy.

Her wide eyes zone in on my skating dress. She stares at the rhinestones, which are now gray and flat. But her eyes brighten as though she can see the sparkle. She reaches a hand out to touch one.

"No name? That's terrible." Who has a kid and doesn't name her? I'd be mad if I didn't have a name. How strange that she's gone all these years without one. I feel as though I need to fix this awful indignity. "How about if I call you Miki? It's a name I wanted for myself when I was little."

"Miki." She repeats the word, exaggerating the *M* sound with her lips. "Yes. That's a good name," she finally announces. "Names are important on Earth."

"What is *this* place?" I ask her.

She wrinkles her nose. "You know, I'm not sure what it's called. Do you want to name it too?"

"No. I want to get out of here."

She smiles as if I've said something dumb. "This is an in-between place."

"In between what?"

"Life and death."

I feel a shudder work its way up my body. "Are you saying I'm . . . ?" My voice breaks. I can't say the word.

"This is where many souls come. They don't stay here, though," she says.

Souls. That word definitely sounds like I'm dead. "This place seems huge. How many 'souls' are here?"

"More than a million people die each week on Earth. Many of them end up here."

She fingers a rhinestone, then touches the fabric of my dress. "I've never seen it up close," she says.

"No. I don't believe you. There's no one else here. Just those people on the other side."

"Oh, them. They're waiting for you."

I'm still trying to take it all in. Am I really dead? Fresh tears fill my eyes. I didn't think I had any left.

"Are *you* dead?" I say in a soft voice, almost a whisper.

She nods. "People die all the time," she says in a cheerful voice, as though it isn't the terrible thing it really is.

When she says that, a memory flashes in front of me, and I'm back in the hospital.

───∧╲╱───

I'm in Grandpa's room. It's dark, and dots of light fill the Milwaukee skyline through the window.

I wasn't allowed to stay long. Hospital rules. The nurses said Grandpa was stable, a good sign. Dad told me to go home and get some rest. I said I wanted to stay, but everyone else said no.

"It's better this way," Mom said. "I'll take you home so you can do your homework."

Mom hugged Dad for a long time and whispered in his ear. Then she handed me a tissue.

"Dry those tears, Eagan. You need to be strong."

I grabbed the tissue. "Why?"

"Because your grandfather doesn't want you to cry for him."

"Yes he does." I crumpled the tissue in my hand. "He wants me to cry and feel just like this."

Dad gathered me in his arms. "It's okay to cry. You two have a special bond."

Mom just shook her head. When we got home, I flopped down on my bed, blew off my homework, and fell asleep with my headphones on. I dreamed of Grandpa bending over his workbench, whistling some made-up tune while he pounded a nail into a bent piece of wood.

"This is what it's all about," he said as he turned the wood over in his hands.

"What?" I asked.

"Life. It's being able to use all your wood, not just the good, straight pieces."

When I woke up, a gray darkness filled my room. Voices floated up from downstairs, and I remembered about Grandpa all over again.

I got up and wiped my eyes, then went downstairs, stopping near the bottom, where nobody could see me. Mrs. Voxler, our neighbor, was in the entryway. She held a covered dish.

"Just my goulash," she was saying. "It heats up real nice at three hundred and fifty degrees."

"It's lovely," Mom said. "I can't thank you enough."

Mom hated goulash.

"How is everyone doing?" Mrs. Voxler asked.

"Richard is a real trooper. Eagan is having a difficult time, though. She didn't realize all the health problems he had."

What health problems? No one ever told me.

"Do you know his prognosis yet? Are they expecting a full recovery?"

Mom's arms were folded. "It's doubtful. Living alone in that big house has been hard for him the last few years, and he definitely can't be left alone now. We'll probably look into a nursing home when he's better. Of course, we have the entire house to go through before we put it up for sale. I dread all that work."

Knowing Mom, she'd start tomorrow.

The rocking chair. She'd see it.

I ducked out the back door and walked the six blocks to his house. I used the spare key hidden under the blue flowerpot and let myself in.

The rocker was downstairs in the basement. I couldn't leave it there, not if they were going to clean out his house. I called Scott and asked if he could come over in his Jeep. Then I sat down at the kitchen table and waited for him.

The silence felt heavy. The kitchen was filled with Grandpa; the leftover smell of bacon. An open package of Fig Newtons. A half-finished crossword puzzle on the table. Half a cup of tea. A bowl of lemon drops in the middle of the table. I put one in my mouth and sucked. I thought of Grandpa's puckered lips.

I half expected Grandpa to be there, to come around the corner tucking in his shirt, carrying the newspaper that he read every morning along with a cup of weak coffee, his glasses perched on the end of his nose.

Then he'd put down his coffee and stick out his hand. "Wanna dance?" he'd ask. He'd move side to side and raise his arms in the air like he thought kids my age danced.

I'd shake my head. "Stop doing that. You're embarrassing me." That would just make him move his arms in an even goofier way. Totally out of synch.

I got up and wandered through the house, stopping to run my hand along the pictures of him and Grandma, to smell the Mennen aftershave on his dresser, to tuck the plaid slippers underneath the end of his bed.

I went downstairs and looked at the tools on the pegboard above his workbench: the wrenches arranged by size; the hammers, clamps, saws, and drills framing the wrenches like a work of art. Grandpa knew every tool from memory, where it hung, and what color handle it had.

Everything was going to change. Without this house, Grandpa would change. Maybe he'd become one of those people in the nursing home who stared out the window and never talked. Maybe he'd become bitter and just sit there and wait to die.

Mom's words still poked at me. She acted as if I was being too emotional about all this. How did she expect me to feel? Grandpa was the one I turned to the most.

She was already planning to sell his house and stick him in a nursing home before the doctors knew how bad he was or if he'd recover. I thought of our house with that empty spare bedroom. It would be perfect for Grandpa. Mom would never even consider it.

It's funny. I'm the one who always worried about the future. When I thought of Grandpa, though, I didn't see him dead or in a nursing home. I saw him living his life, making the most of every day. Always making plans.

It was Mom who could take another man's future and throw it away. Of course, Grandpa knew that about Mom. And he still liked her. He saw such good in her.

Did you have to love your relatives? Mom probably loved me, even with our constant arguing. I guess deep down I loved her too. But I didn't always like her.

I went back upstairs and looked out the window at the darkened street. I didn't know what I was going to do with the rocking chair yet. But it sure wouldn't be here when Mom came over tomorrow to get Grandpa's things.

20

Amelia

His voice floated from the hallway through my open door. He sounded unsure. "Could you ask Amelia if she wants a visitor? Could you tell her it's Ari?"

"No problem," Sara responded. "I'll ask her."

Sara peeked her head around the corner. "A cute guy is here to see you."

"Can you give me a minute?" I was already reaching for a brush.

"Sure." She looked at her watch. "But keep it short. Visiting hours are over in half an hour."

I switched off the TV and brushed my hair. I was so glad Mom and Dad had left for dinner. I hoped they went to a real restaurant, not the hospital cafeteria. I hoped they wouldn't come back too soon.

At least my baby blanket was tucked away. I thought of hiding the horse, but Ari had already seen it. He'd practically stared at it.

My hand shook as I studied my reflection in the mirror. I

wished I was strikingly beautiful like Rachel with her perfect features, her shaped eyebrows, and clear skin. I wished I'd inherited Mom's blond hair and blue eyes, the ones Rachel had somehow gotten instead. My straight brown hair and hazel eyes were so ordinary. A few freckles dotted my nose. Some annoying pimples sprinkled my forehead from the medicine I was taking. There was nothing striking about me except for the scar under my gown. And Ari was here because the social worker sent him, nothing more. He probably thought of me like he thought of Tomas. Just a kid. But I couldn't stop my hands from shaking. I couldn't help feeling excited. I'd never felt this way about a boy before, a boy I'd met for just half an hour.

I was straightening the sheet on my bed when Ari knocked lightly on the wall.

"Knock, knock."

"Hi, Ari."

"You're a hard girl to track down," he said. "I didn't think to look in pediatrics."

The word "pediatrics" made me sound even more like a kid. "Where's Tomas?"

"Home. I was driving by and thought I'd stop in."

"Oh. That's nice." So lame. I definitely didn't know how to talk to a guy.

He took a deep breath. "To be honest, I wanted to talk to you without my little brother around."

My heart fluttered. I searched his eyes, wondering if he was just feeling sorry for me, the poor girl with the bad heart. But then I remembered that I had a different heart now, a healthy one.

His dark brown eyes looked away, as though it had been

hard for him to say that. He had large, serious eyes, the kind that drew attention to them. The kind of eyes I could dream about.

Ari tugged on his button-down long-sleeved shirt, a blue-striped one that he wore untucked over his jeans. I concentrated on the brown locks of hair that swept his collar, while stealing glances at his eyes without being too obvious.

A beeper went off in the hallway. I turned toward the sound, aware that the door was open. I wondered if anyone was standing outside the door listening.

Ari frowned. "There are a couple of reasons I wanted to see you. One is that I could tell you wanted to know more about your donor."

"I do," I admitted.

"So here's the thing. I need to warn you."

"Warn me?"

"To be careful what you wish for."

"Why shouldn't I want to know who my donor is?"

Ari put a hand up. "I'm not saying you shouldn't. But you need to know what you're getting into first. Tomas was lucky. The donor family was great, and Tomas learned a lot about his donor. But you never know what you're going to find when you start digging.

"There was another heart transplant recipient, a kid named Pompilio. He found his donor too. But it didn't turn out so good for him."

"What do you mean?"

Ari pushed the door shut before he spoke. He stepped close. His pants rubbed the side of the bed, and I thought for a moment that he was going to sit down right next to me. His voice was low. "Pompilio's heart came from a girl who was murdered. The family said there was no way they wanted to meet Pompilio, and he became really depressed. Plus, Pompilio kept having these nightmares."

I hadn't thought of that. What if my donor died that way? "That must have been hard for him," I said.

Ari didn't answer right away. "I'm not telling you this to scare you. But after that, Pompilio had a rejection. He's okay now, but I sometimes wonder if that stress caused the rejection."

He shifted up against the bed. "Tomas's doctor said that there's a human element to healing. I wouldn't want this to be a bad experience for you. I wouldn't want it to interfere with your getting better."

Maybe that should have scared me. Maybe that's what he really meant to do, after all. But it had the opposite effect. "You know what it's like when you throw a stone in the water and the waves spread out farther and farther?" I said.

"Yes?"

"Well, that's what's happening to me. I'm getting farther and farther away from myself, and I'm afraid I won't be able to get back. I'm sorry about what happened to that boy, but maybe he would have had the rejection episode anyway. I have a feeling that my donor wants me to find her. It sounds weird, I know."

Ari shook his head. "No. Not weird at all. Tomas said almost the same thing."

"You wanted to warn me. That's why you're here." The flutter of my heart gave way to embarrassment. How could I have thought Ari was interested in me as more than just a heart transplant patient?

His voice faltered. "That was one reason I wanted to talk to you. The other was . . . I could help you find your donor." He looked down. "If you want help."

"Of course," I said, and felt my heart soar again. His voice sounded sincere, and I thought I heard something extra. I couldn't really tell what. Rachel knew about these things, not me.

Mom and Dad came in just then. Kyle was with them, wearing a white surgical mask. They didn't require it here in pediatrics, but Kyle probably wanted to wear one, anyway.

"Meely!" Kyle ran next to my bed then stopped. "How's your new heart?"

"Great. I feel all better," I said, which was mostly true except for the lingering pain down my chest where they'd cut me open. I patted an empty space at the end of my bed with my foot.

Kyle climbed up and sat there, kicking his legs out. He was eyeing the controls next to me. I could tell he wanted to push the buttons. "Aunt Sophie bought me a hamster. His name is Patches."

"I can't wait to see him."

He noticed Ari then. Ari introduced himself to Kyle and my parents. He told them about his brother, Tomas, and how well he was doing. And he said that the social worker had asked them to visit me.

"I was just leaving," he said. "Nice meeting you."

As he turned to leave, Mom's eyebrows shot up. "He's cute," she mouthed.

Ari stopped at the door. "There's one other thing, Amelia."

"What is it?"

"I wanted to ask if I could visit you again."

I felt my face heat up. The first time a guy acts interested in me, and it happens right in front of my parents. "Sure," I said.

Mom winked at me and I rolled my eyes.

"Polite kid," Dad said when he'd left. "Needs a haircut, though."

21

EAGAN

There's a saying in figure skating: *you must either find a way or make one.* If I can land a triple salchow, then I'm not about to let go of my life without a fight. I'm done crying and feeling sorry for myself. It's time to get tough.

"I have to go back. There has to be a way out of here," I say. I walk toward the lighter side of the fog. Miki follows me.

"Where are the other people here? The millions you talked about?"

She gestures around me. "All over. You can't see them?"

I'm wondering if it's the truth. As far as I can tell, there's no one here but me. My voice becomes combative, like when I'm fighting with Mom. "Why can I see you? And why aren't you gray like me?"

She shrinks away. "Are you angry with me?"

I'm afraid she'll leave. Then I'll be alone again. "I'm sorry. It's just frustrating. I don't know what's going on."

She comes back and twirls around, watching the folds in

her dress move in and out in the mist. "I'm here to help you. You asked for me."

I don't remember asking for some frilly airhead girl. I've always been so focused that it's painful watching her act so carefree, as though she doesn't have a worry in the world. As she's twirling, I smell something sweet. It reminds me of blossoming plumerias, the flowers on the lei Mom brought back from Hawaii. It's the first thing I've smelled that didn't belong to one of my flashbacks.

"Do you smell that?"

She sniffs the air and smiles. "Flowers."

"Where's it coming from?"

She points toward the people. "The other side."

Now we're getting somewhere. "Do you know how I get to the other side?"

She points at my life, still flashing in front of me. "I think that's how."

"No. I can't waste any more time looking back." I follow the scent of the flowers. Maybe there's a way across that abyss that I didn't see. A bridge or something.

She follows me. I'm jogging and she's strolling, spending way too much time looking around when all there is to see is gray nothingness. Three times I have to stop and wait for her to catch up.

"I'm probably missing skating practice, and ice time isn't cheap," I tell her, but that doesn't seem to make any difference in her stride. The scent changes as we walk. Now it smells like medicine, disinfectant, bland food, and death. I can't help being drawn to the memory of the last time I saw Grandpa.

"Look, Grandpa. I brought your slippers."

Grandpa nodded. He'd had trouble talking since the stroke because his left side didn't work well. Part of his lip hung down, and that whole side of his face drooped.

That wasn't the worst. He was here, in this place, Scenic Acres, in a twelve-by-twelve-foot room that smelled worse than a hospital room. He was supposedly here to rehab. But we all knew he wasn't going anywhere. Mom had a For Sale sign in front of his house. Did Grandpa know about that? Of course he did. How could he let her do that? How could he still act so upbeat?

I placed the brown loafers next to him on the bed. "Of course, you'll have to get up off your lazy butt to use them."

Grandpa's eyes flashed, and I saw a hint of the man I used to know.

"Tell me the truth," I said as I crossed the tiled floor to the room's one window, which looked out at the parking lot of the church next door. Not what I'd call scenic. Nothing like the lilac bushes and cottonwoods at Grandpa's house. "How are you feeling?"

He motioned me closer and waved his fingers in front of him. "Wif my fingers."

I smiled. I always fell for that joke no matter how many times Grandpa told it to me.

He struggled to speak. "Enjoy ife."

"What?" I said, then immediately wanted to kick myself. I hated to see him screw up his face with such concentration just to spit out a few words.

"Enjoy . . . now. Before . . . you . . . get . . . old."

"Okay. How?"

He shrugged, then made the slow effort again. "Some-time . . . ife . . . sucks."

"Did you say life sucks? Isn't that supposed to be my line?"

Grandpa nodded, and one side of his lip curled up. He was smiling. The first time I'd seen him smile since his stroke.

If I had to live in this place, I'd never smile. But then, I almost never smile anyway.

"It's too quiet in here. Why don't I turn on the radio?"

Dad had brought Grandpa's thirteen-inch TV and propped it on a dresser across from his bed. But before, Grandpa had never watched TV much. He would putter around the base-ment with his tools when he wasn't out walking to the cof-fee shop to meet his friends. Now he'd lost all that. Gone in one paralyzing stroke.

I fiddled with the dial of his radio, the one he'd kept on the corner of his workbench. Flecks of brown and white dried paint made it look out of place on the sterile steel nightstand. I found a station playing big band music.

Grandpa was trying to hold a notepad with his left hand, the bad one. His fingers curled up and out. The skin on his hands was translucent and shiny as he scribbled. He showed me the pad.

Aren't you supposed to be at a dance?

I'd looked forward to the homecoming dance for weeks. It was all I thought about when I wasn't skating. But now it seemed selfish to think about dancing when Grandpa couldn't tie his own shoes. I shook my head. "It's tonight, but I told Scott I didn't feel like going. He's okay with it—he's out in the hall waiting for me."

Grandpa touched my arm. "Bring . . . him . . . in."

I hesitated. "Okay."

It wasn't that I didn't want Scott to meet Grandpa. But I wanted him to meet the Grandpa I knew before the stroke, the one who was strong and independent and good with his hands, who could look at a piece of furniture in a store and go home and make the same thing without taking a single measurement.

I wasn't ashamed of him now, but I still missed my old Grandpa.

Scott wasn't where I'd left him. I expected to find him cowering in a corner, maybe holding his breath in case being old was contagious. Instead he was pushing a woman in a wheelchair down the hallway. What an image. Scott, the big football player, standing behind the hunched-up woman in the wheelchair. And was he ever moving!

"What are you doing?" I shouted after him.

He waved. "Giving Mrs. Solen a ride to the cafeteria. Be right back."

Scott came back while I was browsing through the books Dad had brought Grandpa. A mystery, a book about World War II, and Tom Brokaw's *The Greatest Generation*.

"Hi, Mr. Lindeman." Scott reached out and took Grandpa's right hand. "Nice to meet you."

Grandpa nodded and tried to pull himself up in his bed. He leaned against one side and inched his way up until I helped him find the remote that moved the bed. He took it from me and pressed it until he was almost sitting straight up, then he leaned back against the pillow, exhausted from the effort.

I wanted to tell Scott that this wasn't what Grandpa was

usually like, that Grandpa used to walk two miles a day and had a sharp tongue that matched my own.

Grandpa picked up the pad and showed Scott the same question he'd written before.

"Yeah, the dance," Scott said. "She doesn't want to go."

Grandpa scribbled something underneath his writing. His tongue hung outside his mouth, trailing off to the side as he wrote. Then he spoke as he showed Scott the writing. "Make . . . er."

"Make her," Scott repeated, then raised an eyebrow. "You know Eagan better than I do. Can you make her do anything?"

Grandpa's eyebrows narrowed. I could tell he was up to something. He scribbled for a long time and pulled on Scott's arm. "Try," he said as he showed him the paper, which I couldn't see.

Scott grinned. "Okay. Got it."

"Got what?" I said.

"Nothing." He had a sly smirk on his face.

"Seepy," Grandpa said, lowering himself back down on his pillow and waving his hand at me. "Go now."

"You sneak." I kissed him on the cheek and helped him lower the bed. As we were leaving, I confronted Scott in the hallway. "So what did he draw?"

"Football formation. A rough diagram of an inside trap."

"What does that mean?"

"I think it means he really wants you to go to the dance."

I sighed. "He's always saying I have to enjoy life more."

"He's a smart guy," Scott said.

I thought of the dress Kelly had lent me, a dark blue satin

one with spaghetti straps. Kelly's mom said it showed off my blue eyes.

"I guess we shouldn't let the old guy down. Do you think we can still make it?"

Scott wrapped his arms around me and squeezed. "Hey, it's just a little halftime adjustment."

 **22**

Amelia

"Here," Ari said, handing me a sheet of paper with a phone number printed in big letters. "If you're anything like Tomas, the first month is a big pain in the ass. You can't go anywhere except the doctor's office. You drive everyone crazy because you want to get out. So, if you need someone to talk to . . ."

"Hey," Tomas objected. "I wasn't that bad."

"You were worse."

"Thanks."

I took the paper and tucked it inside my drawing book. I folded a strand of hair behind my right ear, thankful that Mom had decided to run errands when they arrived. Ari had come three times now. He didn't have to come three times. And now he was giving me his phone number. He didn't have to do that, either.

"You promised me food," Tomas said, punching his brother on the arm.

Ari handed his brother a five-dollar bill. "I know how much you miss the cafeteria food. Have at it."

Tomas bent over and clutched his stomach. "Are you serious? You want me to barf?"

"Relax. I saw a sign on the way up here. They're having an ice cream bar today."

Tomas immediately straightened up. "That's different." He took the money and headed toward the door. "You coming?"

"Nah," Ari said. "I'm going to hang here awhile."

"See you later, bro," Tomas said. "Bye, Amelia."

"It's okay if you want to go with him," I assured Ari.

"I'd rather spend time with you." He walked over to the window and picked up the stuffed toy horse Grandma had sent me. "Why don't you have to wear a mask? Tomas had to wear one the whole time he was hospitalized."

"Everyone wore masks the first few days. But now that I'm in a private room with its own air purifier system, they're not as strict. Whenever I leave this room, I have to wear one, though. And no one is permitted to touch me unless they're wearing gloves. Not even my own family can kiss me."

I felt my face grow warm. "Not that anyone else would kiss me . . ." My voice trailed off and I looked down at the covers.

Ari's lips curved upward. "All right, then." He squeezed the horse and tried to make it sit on the end of my bed instead of posed in a standing position. "Why are girls so into stuffed animals?"

"You look like you're having fun with one."

He waved a hoof at me. "I'm horsing around."

"You're really dumb." I laughed and put my hand on my chest. It felt weird to laugh, as if my heart wasn't used to it.

I never thought I'd be able to do this: think about a boy.

No. More than that. Think about flirting with that boy. I always thought about boys. Guys I saw in movies. And cute men like Dr. Michael. But I never imagined I'd get to do anything more. Who'd want a girl with a bad heart?

So I never learned any of that stuff—flirting, kissing. I didn't even know how to kiss. Or fool around—I'd only seen it in movies. It was scary to think about, but when Ari wasn't looking, I stared at his lips and wondered what they'd feel like on mine.

"Hey, don't pull your stitches," Ari warned, but he was smiling.

"No chance of that. All I've done for the last six years is sit around. I can't remember what it's like to do sports or run up a flight of stairs. I don't even remember what it's like to stand in the rain."

Ari shrugged. "It's a lot like standing in the shower. But colder."

"Sounds great to me. Except . . ."

"What?"

"I feel guilty being happy. Like I'm betraying her somehow."

"Her?"

"My donor."

"How do you know your heart didn't come from a guy?"

I pulled on the bedcovers. "Don't laugh, okay? I just know. I feel her inside me. I'm Ameliastein."

"Ameliastein?"

"Part me and part gross experiment. Okay, you can laugh at the Ameliastein reference," I said when I saw him smile.

"So do you have any other borrowed body parts besides the heart?"

I peeked under the blanket. "Nope. Not yet."

"Then you're not Ameliastein."

"But I'm different. The same way you said Tomas was different. I mean, this isn't me. The old me."

Ari nodded. "It was hard to get used to Tomas's new personality. We didn't know what to think at first. And he felt guilty too. That's pretty normal."

"My old self was more like Tomas now. I would never, ever talk back to Mom and Dad. They're probably freaking out, wondering what's going to come out of my mouth next."

Ari smirked. "You gotta keep the parents guessing."

"Sometimes I get really mouthy. I feel like swearing. I never swore once in my entire life."

Ari set the horse down. "Don't take this the wrong way. I kind of like the new you."

I wondered whether Ari would have liked the old me too. Either way, I loved talking to him. He was easy to talk to. I wasn't as shy around him. Not now, anyway. And he made me feel normal.

Once, when I was seven, just after Kyle was born, I picked him up out of his bassinet and carried him to my bed in the middle of the night because he was crying. Mom freaked when she woke and couldn't find him. She yelled at me like a regular mom, one who didn't act as if she had to tiptoe around a sick kid. I think that was the last time she ever yelled at me. The last time I felt normal. I got sick after that.

Ari put the horse back on the ledge. "Okay. So what's the one food you've missed the most since you got sick?"

"I've been sick for six years. I have a long list."

"You can only pick one."

That could be tough. I twisted my mouth, a habit I had

when I was concentrating. "Extra chunky peanut butter," I announced.

He wrinkled his nose. "Peanut butter? I was expecting pepperoni pizza or ice cream."

"That was the first food I had to give up. It was my favorite when I was little."

"You're right," he said, "about one thing."

"I am?"

"Yeah." His brown eyes turned mischievous. "You are Ameliastein."

23

EAGAN

If Miki is here to help, I'll let her, not that it isn't hard. I like being in control, the way I am on the ice. Which makes me wonder: am I that much like Mom?

No, I'm just stressed. I have to relax. I close my eyes and take a long, deep yoga breath, contracting my abdominal muscles. Then I hold the breath and count. Finally, I relax and breathe out through my mouth. Miki is leaning forward, her head cocked, staring at me.

"If there are other people here, why can't I talk to them?" I ask her in a nicer voice.

Miki hovers around me like a firefly. She seems bewildered by everything I do. Her yellow dress stands out like a starburst against the drab gray. The short sleeves puff out against her skinny arms.

"You can. You just don't know how," she says.

She has eyes that remind me of Dad's. They're the same powder blue shade.

"I know how to talk to *you*."

"That's different," Miki says, then puts a finger to her lips. "Shh. Listen."

I don't hear anything except that annoying blur of voices, which could be background noise at any restaurant. I can't make out any words.

"They're praying for you. Here, and on Earth. Do you feel it?"

A sudden glow radiates from inside me. "Is that what this feeling is? I thought it was gas."

She giggles. "Didn't you ever feel that on Earth?"

"Sometimes." I think of gliding around the rink, of doing a perfect sit spin. I think of flushed cheeks and the spray of ice shards. Getting goose bumps, only not from the cold ice. Those thoughts spark something inside me, something warm and substantial, like the girl beside me.

But the competitions don't seem as important now. Maybe it's Miki's carefree attitude rubbing off on me. All that stress over my long program? Wasted energy. Still, I want to go back and do that triple lutz again. Only this time I'd get it right.

That thought sends me back to the ice rink, and the memory wraps around me.

———╱\╱———

"Double salchows are my nemesis," Kelly said as she laced her skates.

"What's a nemesis?" Jasmine hopped from one skate to the other behind Kelly, her dark pigtails flying. She'd just turned ten, the only ten-year-old at our club who'd passed up to intermediate level. Her favorite jump was the double salchow.

"That means it's her hardest move," I said.

"Oh," Jasmine said. "Mine's the double axel."

"Mine's the triple lutz." I played it over in my head, saw myself landing, the edge of my skate gripping the ice. I'd been landing the triple lutz since novice level, but lately I'd started falling, as though I'd forgotten how to do them. The jump that's hardest for a skater fluctuates week by week and sometimes day by day.

"Where's Bailey?" Jasmine asked.

Kelly and I exchanged looks. "She's taking some time off," I said.

"Because she doesn't eat?"

Nothing got past Jasmine. "Yeah, even though she's not a peanut like you, Bailey needs to eat healthier and not get too skinny." Bailey's metabolism would never be like Jasmine's, a little twig of a girl. Jasmine wouldn't have much to worry about when she hit puberty, when most of us found it harder to make those jumps because our bodies were changing and we suddenly had hips and breasts.

Kelly had been a promising skater until she hit puberty early, had a big growth spurt, and never seemed to recover. She was the same level as Jasmine, and really hadn't progressed in the last three years.

I could tell this was Kelly's last year. She had skating goals, but the intensity was gone. The Olympic dream was still intact for the rest of us. We all knew when and where the next winter Olympics would take place and how old we'd be then. We knew who was up and coming in the field, who was injured, and who was retiring.

"I'm not a peanut," Jasmine protested.

"Yeah, you are."

Kelly leaned over and whispered to me, "Did you know Bailey's been anorexic for three years?"

I mouthed a big "no."

"Hey," Jasmine said, grabbing my arm. "I hate when you tell secrets."

Kelly rolled her eyes at me. She didn't like kids much, particularly Jasmine. "It's big-girl talk," she told Jasmine.

"Sorry, peanut," I said. "I hate secrets too."

Especially family secrets. The secret life my parents were living, saying I was an only child when I wasn't, or at least I wasn't supposed to be. There had been a brother or sister once, who'd either died before birth or shortly afterward.

I couldn't remember Mom going to the hospital, but I was only two or three. What happened then, and why didn't they ever tell me about it? Why did they keep it a secret from me all these years?

"Come on, girls," Coach Brian called. "On the ice. Remember, practice doesn't make perfect."

"Perfect practice makes perfect," the six of us replied in unison.

We hurried onto the ice for our group edge class, which focused on our turns and movements and control of our edges. Edge class was the only group activity we had on the ice. The rest of the time we worked with individual coaches.

This was so much better than being home on a Saturday morning. I was never allowed to sleep in, anyway. I loved this place, the smell of the ice, my eyes watering from the cold, the feel of my toes in my skates. I loved grabbing at a mist of cold dust in a beam of light. Jasmine said we were catching stardust. Such a little-girl thing to say, but it made me smile.

This place was my home away from home, and with Grandpa stuck in a nursing home on the other side of town, the people here felt like my closest family now.

Coach Brian worked us hard for almost an hour. Afterward we took a break while Kelly worked with her coach on her short program. She breathed deeply and skated out to the middle, where she took her pose and waited for the music to start. It was a ballad, slow and graceful, like Kelly. Her first jump was a double combination. She made it perfectly.

Sometimes it's the simple moves that you fall on. Kelly did just that. In the middle of one of her backward crossovers, her feet collided with each other, and she tripped and fell forward.

She rolled her eyes. "I can't believe I fell on *that*. Let me start over."

"Come on, Kelly. You can do it," I cheered her on. "Just pretend you're competing." "Keep your head up," I thought. "Arms out straight. Look back during the crossover. Relax, but focus. Oh, and keep smiling, even if you fall. The judges like that."

Kelly struggled with her routine, falling two more times before she made it through. Once we'd tried to count how many times we'd each fallen in one week. It was over forty.

Jasmine pulled on my arm.

"What?"

She waved me down. "Come here."

She cupped her hand close to my ear and whispered, "Kelly has a pimple on her back. But don't tell. It's a secret."

I stood up. "I thought you hated secrets."

"I do. But you tell secrets about *me* all the time."

"We weren't talking about you. We were talking about someone else."

Jasmine folded her arms. "Yeah, right."

"No, really. We were talking about Bailey. About her anorexia."

"Then why were you whispering?"

"Well . . ." I paused. "Because we didn't want anyone else to hear us," I thought to myself. "Because we were gossiping and we knew that Jasmine was a motormouth who repeated everything we said."

"Because we were being diplomatic," I finally said.

"What's diplomatic?"

"Jasmine," her mom called. "I was waiting for you out front."

"Go. I'll explain later," I told her. As I watched Jasmine leave, I imagined what it would have been like to have had a little sister, how my life would have been different. Would I still have felt this desire to succeed? Would Mom have acted differently?

The secret they kept from me wasn't so terrible. The keeping of the secret bothered me more. Why hadn't they ever told me? Or had it slipped out when they were fighting, and I missed it?

Maybe this was like Bailey's secret anorexia that she'd hidden for three years. Maybe some secrets are buried so deep that people forget they're even there.

24

Amelia

It was a simple chair, a wooden rocker. All the pediatric rooms had one. I hadn't paid much attention to it before. It had rounded spindles and curved arms. I stared at it for a long time, as if I knew that chair. The longer I stared, the more I felt it, a strong sensation rising up inside me. I wanted to run my hand over the wood and feel the flow of the grain. I wanted to put my nose up to the headrest and smell the wood and varnish.

I'd never seen the chair before I came here, but I recognized it. How was that possible?

Was it a side effect of the cyclosporine or prednisone? Were the drugs tricking more than just my immune system? Were they causing chaos in my mind as well?

I tried to talk to the social worker. Really, I did. But she kept talking about stuff like guilt and self-esteem. I didn't know how to tell her that my problem went beyond feeling good about myself.

Ari told me to believe in my new heart, to listen to what

it was telling me. His brother had shown me his scar, a reminder that his organ was a loaner from someone else, a person who would always be a part of him from now on.

It made me wonder why God created the heart the way He did, so small a part only the size of a fist but in charge of the whole works. It moved all that blood through the body and never took a rest, even when we slept. Was it any wonder that my new heart made me feel more than just energized now? But that didn't mean this heart had forgotten *her*.

Did that chair mean something? I drew the horse I remembered from my dream in my notebook. I filled in the landscape: silky prairie grass leaning in the direction of the wind with tall buttercups spinning an enchanted walkway for the horse to follow. Pillow clouds reached down to the treetops. I drew the horse running, her mane whipping in the air and her nostrils flared to capture the feeling I'd had riding her. Free. Powerful.

Since the transplant, my body had felt so alive. Everything felt more vivid, even the pain. But the Amelia inside remembered the sick, puffy, tired feeling of the last six years. She had no memory of a heart that beat even and consistent and strong.

Rain splattered against the window. I got out of bed and threw on my robe, then pulled the IV stand with me to the window, where I ran my finger along the drips down the pane. People below were running, covering their heads with newspapers and purses. Mom avoided taking me out in the rain as much as possible. When she did, she dropped me off at the door and made me hurry inside. Now I wished I could stick my head outside and catch raindrops on my tongue, but the window didn't open. I had to go outside. I had to experience that rain.

I unplugged the power cord to the IV and snuck into the

hallway with my IV stand rattling along the patterned linoleum. It was quiet except for the muffled pagers going off and
the hungry beeps of empty IV bags. I made sure none of the
nurses saw me slip into an empty elevator, where I pushed the
button for the ground floor. The elevator jerked down and my
stomach felt queasy.

On the third floor, a woman got on. I smiled and made
eye contact as though I was supposed to be there. She smiled
back and returned her gaze to the closed door. When the elevator reached the first floor, I exited in the opposite direction.

A side door was close by. Three people passed me as I walked
out into the cold rain, dragging my IV stand with me. I stood
outside and looked up into the sky. I stretched out my arms
wide, feeling the cold wetness dribble down inside my robe,
where a large bandage covered my scar. I wasn't supposed to
get it wet. I didn't care.

I splashed my bare feet in a puddle, squished dirt between
my toes. I put my head back, opened my mouth, and felt the
cool liquid slide down my throat.

This felt like life. Not the beeping of a heart monitor
that kept track of how many beats per minute my new heart
could do. What good were beats if you didn't really *feel*
alive?

Fingers tapped my shoulder. "Excuse me, young lady.
What are you doing out here in the rain?"

A woman frowned at me. The name tag attached to her
pink smock read "MS. LANSING."

I shrugged. "Getting wet?" I turned and went back inside.
She followed me to the elevator.

"Where do you think you're going?" she asked.

I pushed the button to close the door. "Back to my room. I

promise." I shivered in the elevator. The air inside felt colder now, and I couldn't wait to snuggle under the covers in my hospital bed.

Maybe Ms. Lansing had put in a call, because there was a nurse outside my room. But I was too tired to stop and explain my wet condition. I walked past her into my room, cleaned myself up, and had just gotten back in bed when Dr. Michael walked in, studying my chart.

"How're you feeling this afternoon?"

I thought of the rain and the chair and the memory that couldn't be explained. I thought of how I'd just gone outside for the first time in over a week. "Good."

He looked up.

"I just got out of the shower," I said, running a hand through my wet hair. "When do I get to go home?"

"How about Tuesday?"

"Tuesday?" As in the day after tomorrow?

He nodded. "We'll take another biopsy before you leave. You'll have to come back once a week at first. Also, the nurses will go over your home health care with you and your parents: what to expect, your regimen of medicine, diet."

"Tuesday," I repeated.

"Only if you want to get out of here." He peered down at me. "From what the nurses are telling me, you've already flown the coop."

His voice was light, but that was all it took for me to regret what I'd done. I hoped my parents wouldn't find out.

As he listened to my heart and examined my scar, Dr. Michael's warm hand brushed my skin, which sent tingles all the way up my arm and down to my fingers. I turned my head away. I imagined what it would be like to be grown-up, to be married to someone like him, to feel his soft hands on my skin in a different way. Then I thought of Ari, of how his hands would feel. But I didn't want Dr. Michael to see all that in my eyes. I focused on the chair.

"You're doing great. Your body is responding to this heart like it was meant for you. No reason to keep you here."

I was ready to go home. "How soon can I go back to school?"

"If everything goes well, you can go back to school in the spring."

School. Back-to-school shopping. Regular activities I'd stuffed away in the back of my mind for so long. Dr. Michael bent over. The dark curl on his forehead made a curly *Q*. I could see under his lab coat, where his shirt hung open, a patch of dark hair. "Can I go on dates?"

Dr. Michael's lips drew up into a smile. "Absolutely. I'll bet you'll be going on many of those. Although you might want to consult your parents on that too."

My cheeks burned and I turned away again. The rocking chair seemed to nod to me as a slight breeze from the vent pushed the air around it.

Dr. Michael touched my drawing on the bed next to me. "You're very artistic. Is that what you want to do when you grow up?"

I tucked the sheets over the picture, embarrassed. "I was just bored."

Dr. Michael lightly patted the covers over my leg. "Well, you have lots of time to decide. And plenty of time for boys."

I picked up my notebook, feeling stupid. All my life, drawing horses had helped to calm me. My fingers automatically knew how to sketch the circles of the basic form, the length of the ears to the nose, the spacing of the legs.

Now all my drawings seemed childish. The rocker moved slightly as though agreeing with me.

"Any concerns?"

"Um, the prednisone. Is there anything else I can take?"

"Why? Are you having problems?"

"A little bit." My face felt hot again and I kept my eyes down. "My face is breaking out." I'd asked the nurses about it. A mild side effect of the drug. There were many worse side effects I could get instead.

Dr. Michael bent down again. "Any rashes?"

"No."

He patted my cheek. "That should go away as we lower the dose. Sometimes it's just a question of maintaining the right level. But we'll stick to a higher dosage for a while."

He wasn't the one with zits popping up on his face. I felt them on my back and shoulders too.

When Dr. Michael stood up, he patted his pocket. He had one of those sports buttons pinned to the outside. A picture of a little boy with dark skin and the same curly hair as Dr. Michael posed on the ice in his hockey gear. His skates were slanted inward. The blades—there was something wrong about them. They weren't the right kind of skates.

My heart sped up. I wanted to reach out and touch that button.

"Any other questions?"

"Can I do sports?" I blurted out.

Dr. Michael raised his eyebrows. "Well, it's something you'll have to work up to. No contact sports. Some of our patients go skiing and swimming. A few play tennis and golf. What sport are you interested in?"

"How about skating?"

25

EAGAN

I swish a hand through the gray murkiness. I'm pissed. "So let's say for the sake of argument that I'm dead. Who dies during a figure skating competition anyway? A car accident would make more sense. I just got my driver's license. But I hit my head on a board. A stupid half inch of board."

Miki tilts her curly head. "Would you have preferred to die in a car accident?"

"Yes. No. I mean, I can't be dead. I don't want to die."

"Most people don't. But you knew you would. Didn't you?"

I want to say no. But here, in this place, you can't lie to yourself. The evidence is flashing all around you in your kaleidoscope memories. "Yeah," I say in a small voice. "Maybe I knew."

"What is this?" Mom asked. I'd just come out of the bathroom and had a towel wrapped around me. She was in my room. She'd discovered my stash. She'd piled the batteries, bars, and bottles of water in the middle of my bed. It was an impressive pile, stacked high like a volcano.

"What are these for?" she said accusingly, confronting me as though she'd found drugs or something worse.

"For an emergency."

"What kind of emergency?"

"End-of-the-world emergency."

"Eagan, you have to stop reading all that crap that makes you do these things."

"It's not the books, Mom. You ever have the feeling that something bad is going to happen? I just want to be prepared."

Mom threw her hands in the air. "What's going to happen? Where do you get these ridiculous ideas?"

I should have kept my mouth shut. But I couldn't help it. "Why are my ideas ridiculous? Because you don't want to hear them?"

"You're sixteen, Eagan. You should be thinking about pleasant things. What about the mental imagery you've been doing for your performances? This," she motioned toward the stack, "can't be helping your mental preparation."

There was a difference between imagining yourself performing your jumps successfully and having a gut feeling about some worldly disaster, but Mom didn't want to listen. "I still have my eye on the goal," I insisted, "but there are other things to think about in the world. I mean, more than the matching pillows on a sofa."

Mom waved the batteries in the air. "Is that what you think I do all day?"

I went tight-lipped and put on my headphones, then turned up the music.

Mom threw the batteries on the bed and stomped out.

The next day I convinced Dad to take me to get my license. I'd passed the written and driving test already. I just had to stand in line and get my picture taken.

"I can miss first period," I said. "It's just a study session."

I wasn't prepared for the twenty-five-minute wait at the license office.

"Do you want to be an organ donor?"

"What?" I flashed a blank look at the woman standing behind the counter. I'd been watching a little kid running in circles around his mom's legs, until he became so dizzy he fell into her arms. She reached down for him at the exact moment he started to fall, as if she had some telepathic link to her child. Is that what all mothers had? Why didn't mine?

The woman behind the counter let out an exasperated sigh, but I didn't flinch. I'd been in line all this time, plus I'd had to stare at the white mustache growing above her upper lip while she ruffled through papers and answered the phone. So what if I got caught not paying attention?

"You didn't check the box for organ donor," she said in a flat voice, as though this was a line she repeated a hundred times a day. She had white hair with crinkly tight curls that looked like they were made of metal. "Do you want to donate your organs if you die?"

"Do they, like, take stuff out of you while you're still alive?" I didn't want them yanking out parts while I still needed them.

She shook her head. Her hair stayed firmly in place. "Definitely not. Here." She handed me a pamphlet about organ donation. "Read this and come back when you decide."

Come back? The motor vehicle office was full. No way was I going to stand in line again.

"No, wait," I protested, pushing back the pamphlet. "I've thought it over already. I want to be a donor."

Her eyebrows shot up over her glasses. "Are you sure?"

"Of course. I'd want to know that through death, I'd saved or enhanced up to sixty lives through organ and tissue donation," I said, reading from the front of the pamphlet.

"Fine. Check the box here," she said, pointing. "You need parental consent if you're under eighteen."

"My dad is outside talking on his cell phone. Can I mark the box and then have him okay it?"

The woman clicked her tongue and looked at the long line behind me. "I suppose, but make sure you bring him back here before you leave so he can give his consent. Otherwise, your license will be held up."

I drew a large check mark, satisfied with myself, even if I didn't like the idea of being a human recycling plant. At least all my parts were in good working order. The man behind me with the cane and droopy eyelids probably didn't have any parts worth donating.

She handed the pamphlet back to me. "In case you want to read it later."

I doubted I would, but I took it anyway. The woman had me sit on a stool to get my picture taken.

The old man behind me winked. "Smile pretty."

He reminded me of Grandpa with his wink, and I felt a small ache in my heart. A month ago, Grandpa could have driven me here. Amazing how much had changed in so little time. I smiled at the man before I sat on the metal stool in front of the camera.

Afterward, I searched for Dad. I found him out front on a bench still talking on his phone. He was using his work voice, so I sat down and waited. I took out the pamphlet the lady had given me. "The Gift of Life." A picture of a little girl riding her bike, her father at her side, highlighted the fact that seventeen people die each day waiting for a transplant. It also stressed the importance of discussing your decision with your family to make sure that they were aware of your commitment.

Discuss your decision with your family? The picture showed people sitting in a living room, the expression on their faces serious but caring. So unreal. If I told Mom I was donating my organs, she'd probably flip.

Our fight yesterday showed me that we could never have a discussion without yelling, and we weren't like the family in that stupid picture anyway. But I felt good about marking the box. I'd decided this myself, a real grown-up decision about my own body and my own wishes. Grandpa would be proud of me.

"Dad," I said, when he'd finished his call, "I want to sign up to be an organ donor on my license. But I need you to sign the consent form."

"Organ donation. That's very mature of you," Dad said as he closed his phone. It was the first time I'd noticed that he had the same receding hairline as Grandpa and the same pale blue eyes. "What made you decide to do that?"

I showed him the pamphlet. "Organ donation is a gift, Dad. And it's free. It won't cost us anything."

26

Amelia

Home! Our white house with black shutters snuggled between two maple trees. The front porch was windswept with gold and brown leaves. The white garage door had dirty basketball marks and a small dent where Mom had accidentally hit it while backing out. Everything looked the same. But nothing really was.

The girl who'd left here ten days ago? She was gone, along with her worn-out heart and purple fingertips.

I couldn't wait to sleep in my own bed, underneath the down comforter instead of those scratchy hospital blankets. I longed to smell the hint of mango that lingered on my bedroom carpet after I'd spilled a whole bottle of body splash on it two months ago. And to be alone in the bathroom—real privacy again! No procedures. No one poking me with needles. A shower with only me in the room, not some nurse being obvious about not looking at my naked body.

As Dad pulled the car into the garage, Mom glanced back.

She had a crooked smile on her lips, as though she wanted to smile and cry at the same time.

"You're going to be surprised," Kyle said. He gave me a sideways grin.

"What's the big secret?"

"You'll see." He covered his mouth so he wouldn't say any more. Secrets were always hard for him to keep.

Kyle and Mom and I had our arms full of plants and stuffed animals. I carried the heart pillow that I was supposed to hold against my chest when I coughed. Dad brought in my suitcase and hospital bags filled with discharge instructions and bottles of pills.

"There's a surprise for you in the kitchen," Mom said when we walked inside.

"I don't like surprises."

"What do you mean? You love surprises." Mom sounded like she was trying to convince me of this.

I'd had enough surprises at the hospital. But I followed her into the kitchen. I almost dropped my pillow. A large banner covered the wall, with "WELCOME HOME, AMELIA!" in bright red letters. Huge pink and red hearts surrounded the writing. On the table was a heart-shaped cake. "WE ♥ YOU, AMELIA" was written across the top. Aunt Sophie and Rachel were there, both smiling a bit nervously, as though they weren't sure how to treat me.

Was it my imagination or did they look at me differently now?

Rachel gave me a fragile hug and handed me a bag decorated with pink ribbons. "It's your favorite movie," she said as I opened it.

"Pretty Woman?" I pulled the DVD from the bag. "Thanks."

Aunt Sophie raised her eyebrows. "Your favorite movie is a Cinderella hooker story?"

"It's her feel-good movie," Mom explained. "The hooker part is just an add-on."

I rolled my eyes. "Why do you have to rationalize it? I can like a hooker movie if I want, Mom."

Mom looked embarrassed. She wasn't used to this new Amelia. But that other girl whose mom would lie next to her on the bed when she couldn't sleep and rub her back seemed so distant. That life was long ago and far away.

Even Aunt Sophie and Rachel looked uncomfortable. It wasn't like me to talk back to Mom.

Aunt Sophie's homemade chicken noodle soup bubbled on the stove and warmed the kitchen. Everything felt familiar but new. Was it just two weeks ago that I was on a low-salt, special diet?

Mom frowned at me. "Are you tired, Amelia? You look a little peaked."

"Kind of," I said, feeling guilty.

Mom nodded. She seemed happier now that I had an excuse for snapping at her.

"You go lie down and we'll bring you some lunch and cake," Aunt Sophie said, taking control of the kitchen.

"Thanks, but I'm not very hungry yet."

"Is it chocolate?"

"No, it's carrot cake, your favorite," Aunt Sophia said.

"I want a piece of cake," Kyle said in a teasing voice.

"Go ahead, Kyle. I don't like carrot cake."

He looked at me funny. "Since when don't you like carrot cake?"

I shrugged. "I don't know. Since now, I guess."

"It's the medication. Side effects," Mom said.

I felt Mom's presence behind me as I headed to the stairs. I turned around. "I'll be fine, Mom."

"I just wanted . . ." Her voice trailed off. She wanted to make sure I got to my room okay. She wanted to make sure I made it up the stairs. Normally, I'd want her behind me. But today I needed to face the stairs by myself, without an audience.

Mom went back to the kitchen, a hurt look on her face.

The stairs. There were marks in the maple finish on the left railing where the chair had been attached, a reminder of my old self. Before Dad bought the electric chair, I'd stare up at the vastness of the stairs and sigh at the effort it would take to climb them. They were beautiful stairs, so spacious and majestic, but like Mount Everest to a kid with a bad heart.

I'd walked up steps at the hospital two days ago as part of my therapy. I'd been surprised at how easy it felt. If I hadn't had a nurse behind me carrying the IV stand that was attached to my arm, I'd have run up them.

Now I took hold of the railing and, like a fairy-tale princess in reverse, glided up one step at a time. I slid my hand along the wood, getting back in touch with the smooth finish and the spots where hands left dirty smudges.

My leg muscles ached partway up, sending little messages to my brain that they weren't used to this yet. My body was still adjusting to this new energy source.

And then I was at the top. I glanced back down at all I'd left behind: The old Amelia who cried because she couldn't play soccer anymore, who moved so slowly, did everything slowly, until she even had to carry a portable oxygen tank on her back when she went out. The old Amelia who died at the hospital when they took out her heart and hooked her up to a heart and lung machine.

Now she was reborn. But my old body didn't feel settled in with the new heart. Who was the new Amelia?

I went to my room and closed the door behind me.

"Hello, room," I said. Everything was the same as before. But why wouldn't it be?

I couldn't help myself. Those pictures on my walls had to go. I hadn't realized that all the horses I drew were staring at me. I took them all down and put them in my closet, then sat down on the bed and stared at the blank walls.

A week ago I'd sat here facing my own death. What was *she* doing a week ago? What sort of pictures were on *her* walls?

Laughter floated up from downstairs. I recognized Mom's laugh. She sounded relaxed and happy. They were celebrating my new heart with carrot cake, while another family was wondering how this could have happened, and why. What was God's plan in all this? Was it so I could get a new heart and live?

It was so unfair. And the worst part? I was happy to be alive. I was happy I had her heart inside me.

The door opened, and an orange ball rolled into my room with a fat little hamster inside, his legs going in fast motion.

"Say hello to Patches," Kyle said from the doorway.

The ball hit something on the floor then turned and shot right. I could barely see the hamster inside as a blur of brown and white whizzed beneath my bed.

It wasn't the hamster that made me cry. It was the bag of

old pill bottles that the hamster ran into at the foot of my bed. The ones that had kept me alive for all those years before the transplant. It was everything tumbling around inside me: gratitude, grief, guilt.

Suddenly it all felt like too much. A sob reeled from deep inside. I tried to keep it down but I couldn't. I'd barely cried since the operation but now I was a blubbering mess.

"He won't hurt you," Kyle said, thinking I was scared of his hamster.

"Amelia?" Mom stood at the door.

"Mommy," I cried.

Mom was inside, running toward me, her arms out-stretched. "Sweetheart, what is it?"

I opened my arms for her, still bawling, and the old Amelia surfaced, the one whose mom made everything better.

27

EAGAN

"I died a virgin," I blurt out. That probably isn't something I should say in front of a kid with innocent-looking eyes. I doubt that Miki even knows what sex is. Still, she's the only one around to talk to.

"I know that sounds like a dumb thing to think about now, but I thought Scott was the *one*, you know, and I wish we'd had more time together."

Miki flutters around me as I talk, almost as if she had wings.

"How can I leave him behind? And Mom and Dad and Kelly. And what about Grandpa? This will *kill* him."

"They'll miss you," Miki says in agreement.

"Scott will forget me," I say dishearteningly.

Miki shakes her head, and the glitter sprinkles down on my gray arms, making my skin sparkle. "He won't forget. Hearts are like stones on an ocean beach," she says. "And people are like the tides that leave permanent marks on them."

"I guess. So what am I supposed to do about him?"

Miki sighs. "I guess you have to let him go."

I turn back to the swirl of my life. "You're pretty smart for a kid. But you really don't understand."

———⋀⋀———

I could barely stand to look at the rocker. Every time I did, I saw Grandpa bending over it, squinting through his bifocals as he rubbed a soft cloth over the varnish.

The chair was in Scott's unfinished basement, underneath a fluorescent light, next to a humming dryer. I circled the chair. I argued with myself, mumbling, "I can't give it to Mom. She stuck Grandpa in a nursing home."

Good point. But another idea, just as strong, made its case: I'd be disappointing Grandpa if I didn't give it to her.

Round and round.

It would be too painful to give it to her now.

Grandpa wanted her to have it.

She doesn't deserve it.

I was getting dizzy.

Scott bounded down the steps, ducking at the end so he didn't hit his head on the low-hanging ceiling. I felt so petite around him. Even when I wore heels.

He put his hands on his hips as he looked down at the chair. "Mom says if you don't take that soon, she's keeping it. She told Dad she wants one for Christmas just like it."

I shook my head. "It's one-of-a-kind."

"Now she's *really* gonna want to keep it."

"Screw that. *My* grandpa made it."

He reached over, grabbed my waist, and pulled me close. "Yeah? Well, it's in *my* basement."

His breath lingered on my neck. I twirled us around,

then pushed Scott down into the rocking chair with me on top.

"Your breath smells good," I said as I laid my head on his chest. I could hear his heart beating, strong and steady, as we rocked.

He lifted my head up to meet his. He kissed me. A soft kiss. Not too fast. Not too slow. I closed my eyes and pretended that kiss would last forever. When I opened my eyes, he was looking at me like he couldn't get enough, like he felt the same way. His blue eyes with tiny brown and green specks made my heartbeat zoom off into warp speed.

Then he kissed me again. Right in the middle of that perfect kiss, I broke away and said, "She doesn't want me dating you."

Scott stared at me. "Who?"

"My mom. She doesn't want me dating anyone. I swear she haunts me. I can't even make out with my boyfriend."

"She's two miles away."

"Not to me she isn't."

I pursed my lips, angry that the thought of Mom's objections to my dating could push into this special moment. But she was everywhere: in our immaculately clean house with the white Italian sofa, even in this rocking chair where I was making out with my boyfriend. God, I wished I could get her out of my head.

"Are you okay?" Scott asked softly.

"Yeah. It's nothing." I shook my head, willing her out.

He traced his finger across my lips. "You're pouting."

"I want to stay here forever."

"Sounds good to me." He kissed me again, then jerked away when a door opened upstairs.

"Scott. You down there? Dinner's ready."

His cheeks flushed at the sound of his mom's voice. "Coming," he yelled.

I stood up. "So much for forever."

His eyes darted between the stairs and the chair. "What do you want to do with this?"

"I have an idea. Come to my house around eight. Bring the rocker."

"Aren't you worried your mom will see it?"

"Sunday night ritual. Mom and Dad go to the movies."

$$\rightarrow\!\!\!\bigwedge\!\!\!\leftarrow$$

At seven fifty-five, I watched through the pleated curtains for Scott's Jeep. He would be on time. He knew Mom and Dad were gone. We had two hours alone.

Just as his red Jeep pulled into the driveway, the phone rang. I pulled the front door open, then ran to answer the phone.

"Mrs. Lindeman?"

"No, this is her daughter. Can I take a message?" Probably a customer wanting to see a house. I grabbed the pen and pad Mom kept next to the phone.

I waved Scott in.

"This is Dr. Sanders's office. She has an appointment tomorrow morning, but Dr. Sanders has been called away on a family emergency. Could you have her call in the morning to reschedule?"

Scott was struggling to hold open the door while carrying in the chair. I watched him as I scribbled down the words, *"Dr. appt. canc. Call to reschedule."*

Why did Mom have a doctor's appointment? Was she sick? My stomach dropped. Even if we didn't get along, I didn't want anything bad to happen to her. Now I felt even more guilty for what I was about to do.

Scott put the chair down in the entryway. "Where do you want it?"

"Follow me." I grabbed two sodas and led the way up the stairs. Our house was one of those turn-of-the-century homes that had been remodeled a million times before my parents bought it when I was a baby. Mom loved the natural wood floors and arched doorways. I loved the extra space between my closet and bathroom. It was a space about three feet wide by three feet across that had been walled in, a sort of hidden room. If I pushed on the back panel of my closet, it opened far enough to fit through.

If I knew that Mom was going to nose around my room, I would have kept my batteries and water and granola bars hidden there, but it's kind of dusty and gross.

I'd pulled out all my leotards, shoes, and boxes from my closet and had them spread out on the floor. I led Scott into the small space. We had to do some maneuvering to get the panel open, but after fifteen minutes of sweaty work, we had a wide enough opening to fit the chair.

I went to get an old blanket to cover the chair. When I came back, Scott was sitting in the rocker.

"Are you sure you want to put this in there? It'll be hard to get out at Christmas."

"I'm thinking of leaving it there permanently."

Scott grabbed one of the sodas. "You and your mom have a real love-hate thing going on, don't you?"

"You don't want to get me started."

He chuckled. "My dad rides me sometimes. I guess he

used to raise hell when he was young, so he worries I'll do it too."

Scott rocked back and forth in the chair like a little kid pushing off on the swings.

"Rocks nice." He looked around the room, taking in the purple walls, the skating posters, and shelves of skating medals and trophies. This was the first time he'd been in my room. His eyes settled on a poster above my bed. It's my favorite skating poster that shows Michelle Kwan in midair.

"That looks like you," he said.

"I wish."

"No, really. That time I picked you up from practice, I couldn't believe how awesome you were. You nailed all those jumps. The other skaters looked at you like you were a freaking god!"

I shrugged. "I work hard at having confidence in myself. I'm not giving up my goals until I see the flash of light in the sky, when the planet is blown to bits because people have screwed things up so bad." That was one thing I liked about Scott. He knew about my pessimism and still continued to date me.

"You ever think of trying to *change* the world?"

I shook my head. "Most of the people I know don't want to hear negative stuff. They prefer to live in denial."

"Not everyone. My brother went to Notre Dame on a football scholarship. Then last year he came home for spring break and said he wanted to be a missionary in Africa."

"What did your parents say?"

"They were floored. But they got used to the idea. Then

he gave me all his football trophies. Said he wouldn't need them in Africa."

I was sprawled out on the end of my bed. Scott looked like he was doing leg presses the way he moved in the chair. He rocked faster the more he talked. I wanted to reach out and touch his arm, but I was afraid I'd break the spell of the moment. He smelled faintly like the weight room at school, where he spent most of his time. He kept talking as he rocked. I couldn't move, I was so mesmerized. I concentrated on the tiny scar on his chin, a gift from our school's rival team during a game a few weeks ago.

"I'd still keep my trophies even if I moved to Africa. I mean, why did he have to give them away?"

"Maybe it was his way of letting go of that part of him."

"Yeah, maybe."

"He might change his mind in a few years. You should save them."

"For sure. I'm not getting rid of them."

I sighed. "You're right. People like your brother are trying to change the world." Did my skating make the world a better place? If I competed internationally next year, would that make a difference?

Suddenly, Scott stopped rocking. "You know, I've never told anyone that before."

He moved forward. I thought he was going to reach out and kiss me, but he stood up. "Your turn," he said, pointing to the chair.

"My turn for what?"

"To talk. In the chair."

"Rocking chair therapy?" I sat down in the rocker and

Scott lay on the bed. He asked me questions and I told him everything as I rocked: how hard I worked at skating, how I had dreams of competing in the Olympics. I told him how I'd found the pictures in the closet, how I didn't get along with Mom, how we argued about everything, even stuff like my competition outfits and the music I picked for skating.

Scott and I had been dating for over two months, but we talked more that night than in all that previous time combined. We sipped our sodas and ran our hands along the rounded edges of the chair, completely absorbed in each other.

After a while, Scott leaned over and picked up one of my skating dresses from the pile on the floor, a shiny silver one I wore two years ago. He raised his eyebrows. "So, are you going to try this on for me?"

"It doesn't fit. I'm thinking of selling some of my old dresses to help pay for travel next year if I compete internationally. Besides," I said, sounding haughty, "figure skating isn't a beauty contest."

"Maybe not, but these dresses are still kind of sexy."

I stood up. "Let's put the chair away now." I covered it with the blanket, and Scott positioned the chair inside the opening. Then we fitted the panel back in place.

"I've decided. I'll leave the chair there for twenty years, like a time capsule. Then I'll take it out and keep it for myself."

Scott sat down on the bed and tugged me toward him. "Come here."

He kissed me and we lay down. We made out awhile before he slipped his hand under my shirt. I wound my leg over his, knowing how vulnerable I was right now, seeing the expression in Scott's eyes. We hadn't made out like this before. Mom would say I was being reckless.

We hadn't noticed the time. We hadn't even heard the back door open and close. It wasn't until the padding of footsteps sounded on the stairs that I realized we weren't alone.

Mom and Dad were home.

28

Amelia

"Just when you think you're alone, you find out you're not."
Tomas looked at me when he spoke, as though I was the only
one in the room. His voice was almost a whisper. "You have
your family and all the people in the transplant program
pulling for you. And if you're lucky, you've got the donor
family too. For me, well, I *had* to know who my donor was. I
couldn't get on with my life until I did."

A few chairs squeaked against the tile floor. The overhead
lights hummed brightly above us. We were seated in a circle
in the center of the room. The facilitator, Mrs. Keely, held her
hands on her lap in a neat pile. Her feet were tucked together
behind the leg of her chair. She peered at us above narrow
slits of glasses connected to a green chain around her neck.

Mom and Dad were in another room talking to other parents whose kids had transplants. I could hear the sound of
voices rising and falling, even some laughter. It was quieter in
here. Too quiet.

Mrs. Keely finally spoke. "Did you find closure in meeting the donor family?"

Tomas shrugged. "What do you mean?"

"Did it help you move on with your life?"

"Oh, yeah. It did. Kind of like my friend Jake, who found out he was adopted. He felt like he wasn't whole until he knew where he came from. I felt that way, only about my heart."

I wanted to say something encouraging to Tomas, but my voice couldn't find its way out. I'd always had trouble speaking in a group.

Another kid shook his head. His mouth was set in a straight line as he stared down at the square tiles.

"You don't feel that way, Jackson?"

"No way. I don't want to know nothing about my donor. I've got enough to deal with: school, friends, meds, rejection. Don't need to add that to my situation."

Mrs. Keely nodded. "Even though Tomas met his donor's family, most donors don't make contact. And just as we have differing opinions on this, we also have to keep in mind that not every donor family is going to want to meet the transplant recipient. For some, it's too painful."

No one said anything for a long time. Mrs. Keely cleared her throat. "Perhaps we should go over the list of symptoms of a rejection." She read from a card. "Frequent cough, sweating or chills, pain or difficulty breathing, change in color of lips, hands, or feet. Nausea or diarrhea, chest pain, skin rash, vomiting, temperature more than one hundred degrees, sores or blisters on mouth, yellow color change in whites of eyes, puffiness or swelling of eyes, hands, feet, or legs. Anything else to watch out for?"

"How about sudden death?" Jackson said. "That's a sure symptom of rejection."

A nervous laugh spread among our group of six. Only three of us were heart transplant patients. Two others were kidney transplants and one was on the waiting list for a heart.

Mrs. Keely wasn't smiling. "Because this is our first meeting, I want to be open to whatever *serious* subjects you want to talk about, such as rejection or medications. Does anyone want to add to what Tomas or Jackson talked about?" Another long silence.

"Well," Mrs. Keely said, and now even she seemed uncomfortable because of the quiet.

"I want to know who my heart donor is," I blurted out, my voice louder than I intended. The sound echoed off the walls. "I think she liked to skate."

Mrs. Keely's eyebrows shot up. "How do you know that?"

I'd spoken. I'd revealed more than I wanted to. But I couldn't help myself. My voice was strong and determined. "Tomorrow will be a month since my transplant, and I keep discovering new things about her. I saw a photo of a hockey player, and I had a weird feeling. Then last week I saw figure skaters on TV, and it just clicked. Those sparkly dresses and icy spins made my heart jump." I hadn't even told my mom and dad about it, and here I was confessing to a group of strangers.

"And finding the donor family: this is something *you* want to do?"

"Yes. Well, I don't expect them to be like a second family or anything. I just want to meet them for the same reasons that Tomas did. And I want to thank them in person for what they did."

I looked at Tomas, who was cracking his knuckles and nodding at me.

"And how do you think this will help *you* move on?" Mrs. Keely asked, removing her glasses.

I saw the disbelief in her hazel eyes. She didn't approve, I could tell. But I had to say what was on my mind. "It isn't for me. It's for her. She needs me to meet them so *she* can move on."

 **29**

EAGAN

It's as though someone has adjusted the lens of a camera into focus. I can see the woman in the purple dress across from us. She's waving at me. I wave back. She has gray hair, although I still can't see her facial features. I know her from somewhere. She's so familiar, but I can't place her.

Suddenly, I'm overcome with an inexplicable sadness.

"Does everyone leave this place?" I ask Miki.

"Eventually. Some will be here a long time, though."

"How long?"

"A hundred years. Or longer than that."

I shiver. "Will I be here that long?"

"No. You'll hardly spend any time here."

Maybe because I died so young? "They must have had long lives to spend that much time looking back."

She shakes her sparkly head. "It's not how long they lived. It's *how* they lived. Some have trouble reconciling themselves to that."

"I wish I could talk to her," I say as I watch the woman across from us.

"You will soon," Miki says. "Don't give up hope."

I notice that, now, my dress has splotches of plum and a bit of gold color too. And the fog continues to lighten and break apart. Maybe there is hope, after all.

———⋀⋁———

Scott jumped up off the bed. I was still straightening my shirt when Mom rounded the corner and let out a small gasp. Dad was right behind her.

"What the . . ."

"Dad." I stood up. "You remember Scott."

Scott's ears turned red.

"Don't you have a competition tomorrow? Weren't you supposed to be studying?" Mom demanded. "Where are your books?"

Books. I'd forgotten. Mom would never believe we'd been just talking for three hours.

Scott moved toward the door. "I gotta go. Nice to see you again," he said as he inched his way around my parents.

"I'll see you out," Dad said. "Cheryl, you talk to your daughter." He closed the door and went downstairs.

I listened for their voices. I was worried about what Dad would say. I *knew* Mom was going to explode. I was ready for it. But Dad, I wasn't sure about. He usually kept his anger below the surface.

Mom's face was already turning shades of red. She spoke through her teeth. "What was he doing in your room? Don't you know any better?"

"We weren't doing anything."

"Listen, young lady, you're sixteen years old, and we can't even trust you while we go out for a movie." She stopped and stared at the mess of shoes and clothes on the floor. "Where did *this* come from?"

"My closet. I was cleaning."

"You had a boy in your room, and you want me to believe you were cleaning your closet?"

"You should try it sometime. It's amazing what you might find in the back of a closet." My voice was defiant.

Mom looked puzzled, as if she didn't know what I was talking about. How could she forget the pictures she'd hidden?

"I saw the pictures, Mom. The ones in the box at the back of your closet. Pictures of you pregnant. And not pregnant with *me*."

A slow realization spread across her face. "Eagan, why didn't you tell me?"

"Why didn't *I* tell *you*? Why didn't *you* tell *me*?"

The reddish shade on Mom's face had paled. She sat down on the edge of my bed and closed her eyes. Finally, she looked up at me.

"You're too young to understand, Eagan."

"Mom, girls my age get pregnant. How am I too young?"

She put her hand to her temple. "I guess we should have told you. But you were so young. You didn't remember. You never said anything."

"Why tell me I was an only child?"

"It was easier."

"Easier than the truth?"

"I was five months along; it was a late-term miscarriage. It made more sense not to make a huge deal about it."

"Did you have a memorial service?"

"No. We didn't think it was necessary."

"So if *I* die, will you think it's necessary?"

"For God's sake, Eagan. Can't this discussion wait?"

"No, it can't."

Mom was shaking her head the way she always did when she thought I was being impossible. "Fine. I was raised to be thankful for what I have. I had you, Eagan. And even though I loved that baby and desperately wanted another child, I was thankful that I had a beautiful daughter, a wonderful husband, and a nice home. Is that so terrible?"

I let out a small breath. Grandpa said Mom had a hard shell. I wanted to crack it open, to find out what was really underneath. But this was the most she'd ever opened up to me.

"No, I guess not."

Mom reached over and put her hand on my face. Her voice grew soft. "Maybe that's why I have such tunnel vision about your skating. I want so much for you, Eagan. You're all I have."

Mom looked down and put her hand on her stomach. She opened her mouth like she was going to say something more, but then she stood. "You need your rest. Go to bed. We'll discuss that boy later."

"Mom, just one more question. Was it a boy or a girl?"

She paused in the dark hallway.

"A girl."

Then she was gone.

I couldn't sleep that night. I didn't understand my mother. I didn't think I ever would. My body felt drained from the effort. I was exhausted, but my brain continued working overtime, unable to let it go.

Would I ever keep secrets like that? Then I looked at my

closet, where hidden in a tiny space was a rocking chair that was supposed to go to Mom. How was that any different?

I couldn't keep the chair from her. It wouldn't be right. I'd get it out before Christmas and give it to her just like Grandpa and I had planned. Otherwise, I might turn out just like Mom, and the chain of secrets would continue with me.

It was two in the morning when I went downstairs to the living room. I imagined the rocker there, in front of the window in a slit of light that peeked through the blinds. I sat down across from that space and dreamed of another family with two children. They played on the blue plaid sofa and built forts together with the cream-colored crocheted blanket.

And they were happy, this other family. If that family's grandfather had a stroke, they'd take him in and nurse him back to health. Because they had the mom with the kind eyes and soft voice. The one who came like a gust of fresh air and disappeared just as quickly. She was the mom I longed for. The one I loved.

I fell asleep in the living room, dreaming of this other girl and this other family. The family who loved the handmade rocking chair and made it the centerpiece of their home.

30

Amelia

Ari's voice sounded older on the phone. "First, write down everything you know for sure."

I spoke softly, even though my bedroom door was closed. "I don't know anything for sure."

"Yes you do. You know when your transplant took place. That's a start."

I wrote down the date in my notebook. "What else?"

"Now write down what you *might* know. You think it's a girl, right?"

I wrote that down with a question mark. "What about location?" I asked. "I don't know where she lived."

"The heart could have come from anywhere. We also don't know the donor's age, but your mom said the donor was a teen with a driver's license, so she had to be at least sixteen."

I wrote down sixteen with another question mark. "This is hopeless."

"Hey, I love a good mystery."

"This mystery doesn't have any leads."

"Maybe your donor died unexpectedly. So we'll search for teen accident deaths, that sort of thing."

I opened my laptop and typed in "teen accident." "Only seven million, one hundred and twenty thousand results. This won't take long at all."

I could hear Ari typing on his laptop. "Keep narrowing. Search by date," he said.

I typed in the date and the word "accident." I opened a site that showed a Nissan wrapped around a telephone pole. That poor teen didn't have a chance. But I clicked on it and found out that the teen hadn't died after all.

"What now?"

Ari's voice was optimistic. "Try using your gut instinct."

"I have a gut feeling she liked figure skating." I typed that in. Only five million, eight hundred and ten thousand hits. I clicked on a couple. Duds.

Ari's typing was like a horse racing around a track. Mine was like a slow trot. A minute later he suddenly stopped. "What about . . . Just a sec. God, it can't be this easy."

"What? What did you find?" My heart sped up.

"Type in 'figure skater death.' "

I typed the words and hit the enter key. A page on the death of a former figure skater who died of a drug overdose. The death of an eighty-four-year-old former figure skater. The death of the Ice Capades.

"I don't see anything, Ari."

"It's on the third page."

I clicked to that page. The fourth entry read "Local Skating Coaches Address Starburst Invitational Death."

I clicked on that one. The article was dated October 27, three days after my transplant. I read the article about the safety concerns following the death of a sixteen-year-old Wisconsin girl who hit her head on the boards during a skating competition.

"Did you see it?" Ari's voice was careful. "When she died?"

I kept reading. Her accident happened the night before my transplant. She never regained consciousness and died the exact same day as my transplant! Then I came to her name, and my heart sped up as if it recognized her. "Eagan Lindeman."

"It's her! The date . . ."

"Could be a coincidence. You can't jump to conclusions."

"She was a figure skater, Ari. Maybe there's a reason we found her so easily. Maybe she wanted us to find her."

"Whoa. You don't even know if she was a donor. People die every day, Amelia."

"How do I find out for sure?"

"There's only one way. You have to call them and ask."

My stomach lurched. "Me? I can't just call up and say, 'Hi, I'm sorry about your daughter, and by the way, did she happen to donate her heart because I think I have it?'"

"Well, I was thinking of something more subtle, but yeah. That's about the way it went for Tomas. It took about a week for him to get up the nerve to dial their number."

"I'm not gutsy like Tomas."

He sighed into the phone. "*You* should call them."

"I can't."

There was a long silence. "Okay. I'll do it."

My voice cracked. "I owe you big time."

"Don't thank me yet. They may not want to see you."

"I know. But *she* wants me to see them."

"Only transplants can talk that way without sounding freakin' crazy. I'll call you back after I talk to them."

I hung up and waited by the phone. A while later, Mom knocked on my door. I pretended I was reading.

"What do you want?" I called.

She opened the door. Mom had my meds and a glass of juice and a croissant sandwich and chips balanced in both hands. "You know, you always left your door open before. What's with this sudden need for privacy?"

I shrugged. "It's too noisy." Which was a lie. Kyle was at his friend's house, and I could barely hear the TV downstairs. Mom set the food and pills down on my desk and glanced around as though she'd forgotten what my room looked like. I hoped Ari didn't call back while she was here. I stuck my head back into a mystery I'd been reading. Now the words blurred before me. I had my own mystery to solve.

"Who was on the phone?"

"Ari," I answered behind the book.

"That boy who visited you in the hospital?"

"Uh-huh."

"What did he want?"

I had to look up then. I kept my voice even and my eyes calm. "To talk to me."

"Oh," she said, and I could hear her disappointment. She wanted me to tell her everything. Normally I would have. Mom walked toward the door. "Do you want me to keep it open?"

I shook my head. "Close it when you leave." She frowned, then turned and walked out, closing the door behind her. I heard her footsteps on the stairs.

I opened the laptop and read the article again. Eagan was my donor. I just knew, like I'd known she was a figure skater, like I'd known she was a teenage girl.

I swallowed my pills with the juice, wondering why some pills couldn't have helped Eagan instead. How could one teen survive a car crash around a telephone pole and another die from hitting her head?

I ate a few bites of my croissant and read the article two more times, then looked up her obituary in the local Wisconsin newspaper where she'd lived. There was a black-and-white photo of her. I inhaled a sharp breath. There she was—a thin, oval face with long, dark, curly hair and intense eyes that almost made you uncomfortable. More than gorgeous. She was stunning. I ran my fingers across her picture on the computer screen. Accomplished. Beautiful. She was everything that I wasn't.

I continued reading. She was survived by her parents, Cheryl and Richard, and her grandfather Calvin. Eagan was a sophomore in high school and a promising skater. She was an only child.

How would her parents feel about meeting me after they'd lost their only child? If they decided to meet me, would it be to search for their daughter in me, to hope for some recognition?

I paced the room for fifteen minutes, then picked up my drawing pad and sketched the horse I'd ridden in my hospital dream. I rarely remembered dreams, but this one had been vivid.

I don't know how much time passed. When I'm drawing, I lose all sense of time. But it calmed my nerves and gave me something to do with my hands. Otherwise, I'd have been pulling my hair out.

I grabbed at the telephone on the first ring. "Please," I whispered, "let it be him."

"Amelia?"

"Ari?" Then Mom picked up the other phone. "I've got it, Mom," I said in a hurried voice. We were both quiet until we heard her click off.

"You alone now?"

"Yes. Did you talk to them?"

"No. I got their answering machine, but I didn't think this was something we'd want to leave as a message."

My heart dropped. "No, of course not."

"I have to go now. I'll try again after school tomorrow."

"Sure." That seemed so long from now.

"Promise me one thing," he said. "Don't get depressed no matter what."

"I won't," I said, wondering if I could keep that promise.

———∿———

Five days later, I was more than depressed. Ari had called two more times, and still no one had answered. I wondered where Eagan's parents were and why they weren't answering their phone. Ari had promised to call again last night after he helped his dad hang Christmas lights, but then it had gotten too late. This wasn't turning out to be as easy as I'd thought.

Dad was downstairs filling out insurance paperwork. Kyle was at school. Mom was Christmas shopping. I was supposed to be reading my social studies book, but all I could think about was that phone call.

I had written the phone number inside my notebook in small print. I stared at the number, wondering if this was a good time to call, if there would *ever* be a good time. I picked up the phone and put it back down. I picked it up again and dialed the number then hung up before it rang.

Should I wait for Ari or just do it myself? I couldn't bear waiting another day. If I called, what would I say? My stomach rumbled. I felt queasy and hungry at the same time, as though my stomach was as indecisive as I was.

I took a deep breath and dialed the number. This time I didn't hang up.

"Hello?" A deep voice answered.

"Uh . . . hi." He'd picked up on the first ring. Maybe this was meant to happen after all. "Mr. Lindeman?"

"Yes. Can I help you?"

"I hope so." There wasn't an easy way to ask my question, and I didn't have time to come up with one now. "Was your daughter a heart donor?"

He didn't answer. There was a distant noise like someone blowing their nose. Was he crying? Then he cleared his throat. "Are you Amelia?"

I let out a small cry. "How did you know my name?"

"We received your letter last week."

Hearing it out loud made my heart jump. It was really her. How did they get my letter so soon?

"I'm really sorry about your daughter. I wondered if I could meet you, if that's okay. I live in Minnesota and I'm not that far away and I was just hoping that you'd talk to me and let me visit." I was rambling on, wanting it so badly but needing to say the right thing, if that was possible.

"To be honest, it's been very tough, Amelia. I should probably discuss this with my wife first."

"I understand," I said. My voice sounded so sad. "I could make it a short visit."

He sniffed. "I can tell this is important to you. You know what? I'd like to meet you. I'm sure this will be good for Cheryl too. Whenever you're up to traveling."

For a moment I was speechless. He wanted to meet me. There was a reason I'd called and it was coming together now. I recovered my voice. "Next Saturday. I'll be there next Saturday."

"I look forward to it," he said. "We'll see you then."

I put down the phone and sank onto my bed. I'd really done it. But now what? If I asked my parents to take me, they'd make me wait another six months, or else they'd just say no to the whole thing. Sometimes you know in your heart that you're doing the right thing, even though it means lying to your parents.

Now I had plans to make and lies to come up with. And I had one more call to make. I had to convince Ari to take me.

31

EAGAN

"I don't want to be stuck here for another minute," I complain. "Is there any way I can go back to my life?"

Miki shakes her head. "Not the same way as before."

"But there's a way?"

"Listen," she says. She takes my hand and for just a few seconds the mist vanishes and I can see across to that beautiful field of clover and multicolored flowers stretching out toward the grassy hill. And I recognize the woman in purple who was waving before. It's my grandma. She's sitting in the grass and swaying to music that's floating out from beyond the hill.

This music is different from any I've ever heard before. Not a choir of angels or a symphony or even a harp. A single voice. One perfect voice. This is way better than gold streets and pearly gates.

"Can I go there?"

"Sure. When you're ready to leave your life behind."

Easier said than done. But that voice is like the most perfect jump in skating history. It's like silky chocolate pudding sliding down my throat, like a perfect kiss, like every single thing in my life that was good. It makes me forget every pain, disappointment, or heartache I ever had.

And seeing Grandma in that beautiful field is so tempting, especially since I'm surrounded by gray. Every color is eye candy, brighter than I thought possible.

Maybe dying young isn't as awful as I'd thought. I had a good life, something I didn't always see when I was alive. But there were moments when I recognized it. Like my last conversation with Scott.

Scott grabbed a book out of his locker. "I hate missing your Invitational. Sure you're not mad about it?"

I pushed Scott into his locker. "No, dummy. It's your football banquet. I can't ask you to miss that. Besides, I have lots of upcoming competitions that will bore your socks off."

"Nah." He grabbed me and turned me around, and before I could react, I was pinned against his locker. His strength always impressed me. I had strong legs from skating every day, and I lifted weights for my arms, but they were never a match for his. His shoulders pressed closer and he spoke softly in my ear. "How can I ever be bored when I'm watching you skate around in that sexy little dress?"

I felt my face flush. Just his voice had that effect on me. I was in way over my head with this guy. The hallway was packed with students, but I zoned out all the voices except Scott's.

I remembered the homecoming dance, how he'd slipped a corsage on my wrist made of miniature white roses, how he'd made me feel as if I was the only one on the dance floor, and how he'd kissed me three times that night, each kiss more lingering, each one just as soft as the petals on my corsage.

Okay. I hadn't ever had a boyfriend before. Maybe we were still in that "honeymoon phase," because we hadn't had a single fight yet and I never felt bored or tired of him. How likely was it that I'd found my soul mate on the first try?

"So what did my dad say to you last night?"

Scott shrugged. "He was cool. He didn't ask me what my intentions were or anything like that. Just told me that they prefer that we stay downstairs when they're gone. Better than my dad would have been. He'd have gone berserk."

I smirked. "That's my mom's specialty."

"Sorry. You got stuck with her. Did she ground you?"

"Uh, no." It struck me then that she hadn't punished me. Had she forgotten or was she saving it for later? I'd left early this morning, before she'd come down. What would she have said if she'd found me asleep on the living room floor?

Scott raised his eyebrows. "You know, you gripe about her all the time, but she doesn't sound so bad."

I sighed. "She's hard to explain. Skating is the one thing that binds us together. If it weren't for that, I don't know how we'd survive each other."

Scott pulled back, but ran a finger across my cheek, and I felt the familiar rush from his touch. "So, your mom didn't ground you, and your dad didn't seem too mad. Then we're still on for Friday night?"

I gave him a sideways glance. "That depends. What *are* your intentions?"

The bell rang. Scott grabbed a book from his locker and flashed me a sexy grin before he left. "My intentions are to hit you with a power sweep before you get a chance to trade me. I'm not a free agent, Eagan. I'm a franchise player."

Scott gave me a quick kiss and walked off to class. I had no idea what he'd just said, but it sounded sweet.

Several girls were watching us, a look of envy in their eyes. I was so damn lucky. I had an awesome boyfriend who was as crazy about me as I was about him. I had a future in a sport I excelled at, a sport I loved.

I thought back to when a local reporter had done a story on me when I'd won the State Novice title. She wrote that I was making a huge sacrifice to skate, but I didn't see any sacrifice at all. Skating was my life. Not until I'd met Scott did I begin to rethink that idea. The good part was that Scott supported me. He wasn't jealous of my skating time and commitment. He understood.

And I got to see Scott every day at school and do something I loved afterward. Not too shabby.

I sprinted to class. The halls looked brighter than before and people acted friendlier. I thought of Grandpa, of how he could still be upbeat even when he was living in a nursing home, drinking through a straw with his droopy mouth while half of his body was totally useless.

I even had hope for Mom. Maybe someday we'd have more than skating to bind us together.

For now, skating was enough. I skated pretty darn good, come to think of it. I'd skate my best tonight, and if Bailey dropped out of Nationals, I'd skate my best there too. My parents would always be behind me in skating. And I still had Grandpa and Scott and my friends. Maybe the future wasn't as bad as I thought.

 **32**

Amelia

"I told you this would happen," Mom said. "I just didn't think it would happen so soon." Her hands were clasped together just below her chin.

I stood between Mom and Dad as they pondered this life-altering moment.

"Our little girl is going on her first date," Dad said, shaking his head.

Mom put her hand on my shoulder. "Now, you'll be careful, won't you? You have your mask with you? And sit away from the crowd. Maybe up front. Most people don't sit in the first few rows."

"Ari said the matinee is never crowded," I told her. "And the movie has been in the theater for three weeks already." I'd rehearsed these lines in front of the mirror. But guilt has a way of making everything sound faked. I looked away from Mom in case she could tell I was lying.

The knock on the door was a relief from my parents' watchful eyes.

Dad ushered Ari in. He extended his hand and Ari responded with an enthusiastic shake. "Nice to see you again, Mr. Monaghan."

I put on my coat.

"You'll be home around five?" Mom asked, even though we'd been over this ten times already.

"Yes," Ari said, looking at me for confirmation. His eyes didn't show anything except politeness. Ari obviously excelled at being polite.

I was too nervous to say anything.

"Don't overdo it, Amelia. If you get tired, come home right away."

"I will," I said in a soft voice.

"Well, good-bye," Mom said. I couldn't look at her. I couldn't pretend that I wasn't about to betray Mom's trust. I was going to cause her such worry, after all she'd been through already.

"Have a good time," Dad said.

Two years ago, I watched from our front window as Brea Taken and her prom date posed for pictures across the street on her front lawn. I remembered how her dress sparkled as it caught the light, how they stood in front of the maple tree and posed, looking a little uncomfortable, as though they couldn't wait to get this obligation over with so they could get on with the fun part.

Now I knew what that felt like, except that I had to remind myself that this wasn't a real date. But as I inhaled Ari's clean hair and soap smell, I couldn't help but imagine us in a darkened theater, our arms brushing each other and his hand pressed into mine.

Ari opened the car door for me while my parents watched

from the window. I felt their eyes on us as I put on my seat belt, as Ari got in and put on his seat belt, and as he started the car, checked the rearview mirror, and slowly pulled away from the curb.

He turned right at the corner as though he was heading toward the movie theater at the mall. But instead he turned left at the next corner toward the interstate.

As he pulled up to a stop sign, his car made a loud sound like a lawn mower. "I need a new muffler," he said sheepishly. He reached over and opened the glove compartment, taking out the directions he'd printed. He handed the paper to me. "You can navigate. Make sure I don't take any wrong turns."

"Okay." I had a feeling he already knew the way, but it was something to keep me preoccupied.

I noticed that the rearview mirror on my side was held on with duct tape. Ari had said his car was a beater. He wasn't kidding.

The inside of his Honda Civic was clean, even if there was a small rip in my armrest. I leaned back and looked out the window at the bare trees waiting for a blast of December snow to give them color. This was the first time I'd ever been out without an adult watching over me. The first time I'd been in a car with a boy. We had a five-hour drive, each way. What do you talk to a boy about for five hours?

But even nervousness couldn't stop the feeling of freedom from sinking in. I had ten unchaperoned hours with no one checking on me or poking me.

The Honda moved away from the stop sign, but Ari suddenly slammed on the brakes.

"Your medications," he said, as though he'd just thought of it.

I patted my bulky purse. "I brought the ones I need. I already took eleven pills this morning. My dose of prednisone, the blood pressure meds, infection meds, statin drugs, magnesium supplements, and aspirin are once-a-day pills. I won't need to take them again until tomorrow morning, and we'll be back before then."

Ari stepped on the gas again. "What are your parents going to say when you're not home by five?"

"I don't know. I've never done anything like this before. I guess they'll be mad."

"I have my cell phone if you want to call them."

"I don't think I can handle that until I've talked to Eagan's family. I left a note on my bed, because Mom will notice the pills are missing." She kept them lined up on the kitchen counter. They stretched across the entire length of the counter like a row of Kyle's army men, ready for action.

"I didn't tell them in the note where I was going, just that I planned to meet my donor's family and would be home late."

Would Mom check my room and find the note? Maybe I should have left it in a more conspicuous place.

I'd calculated a five-hour trip to Milwaukee, a couple of hours to meet Eagan's family, an hour for restroom and food stops, and another five hours back to Minnesota. That would put us home at one o'clock in the morning. I'd never stayed out that late before in my life.

Ari frowned. "I don't want your parents to hate me, Amelia."

"I'll tell them I made you do it."

"Just the same, they'll probably never let me see you again."

"That won't happen. I won't let it," I reassured him, although I didn't know how I'd pull it off. I liked the sound of

Ari's voice when he said it, though. At least he did want to see me again.

"What about you?" I asked. "Will you get in trouble with your parents?"

He shook his head. "I doubt it. I've spent whole nights in the garage working on my car, and no one came out to check on me. Tomas has taken so much of their attention the last couple of years that I've gotten used to taking care of myself."

I thought of Kyle, of how he must have felt when Mom missed his baseball games because of me.

Ari looked over at me. "Don't get me wrong. I'm not complaining. I know that Tomas didn't ask for his problems."

"But you need to be noticed too."

He shrugged. "I do okay."

"Maybe," I said. "Maybe not."

Ari smirked. "What's that supposed to mean?"

"You probably wouldn't be hanging around hospitals if it weren't for Tomas."

"That's true," he conceded.

"Thanks again for taking me," I said. I'd already thanked him more times than I could count, but it never seemed enough. "I didn't have anyone else to ask."

We were going down a side street when Ari looked over at me and slowed down. "Hey, could you take the wheel for a minute?"

"Me? I've never . . ."

"Here." He put my left hand on the wheel. It moved and the car wriggled back and forth. I grasped the leather grooves tightly, trying to keep the car in a straight line while Ari searched his pants pockets. I was steering. It was scary. And exciting.

"There's a curve up ahead," I shouted.

"Got it," Ari said, taking the wheel from me.

I let out a nervous laugh. It was kind of fun, after all.

Ari handed me a slip of paper. A phone number was scribbled on it.

"Eagan's parents' number. In case you chicken out," he said.

"I won't." But even as I said it, I wasn't sure.

We reached the interstate and I felt both regret and excitement mixing with the essential meds that kept Eagan's heart beating in my chest. This journey had started out as a dream, and now it was really happening. Flashes of sunlight hit my eyes until we turned east toward Milwaukee.

Traffic was busy, and Ari had his hands full keeping up with the white minivan ahead of us. He motioned toward the backseat. "I brought along some sandwiches and sodas in case you're hungry."

"I'm starved." I reached into the back and opened a plastic bag. The smell of peanut butter wafted up. "You remembered!"

"Not just peanut butter," Ari said. "Extra crunchy peanut butter."

I took out a sandwich and a soda. "This is great."

Ari smiled. "You're the only girl I could impress with a peanut butter sandwich."

"It's not just the sandwich. It's the thought behind the sandwich."

"No big deal," Ari said.

"It is a big deal. I've seen how you are with Tomas. You're like his best friend instead of his brother. And you volunteer at the hospital with him when you could be off doing your own thing."

Ari pushed his hair behind his right ear. "Okay, now I feel like a jerk."

"Why?"

"I only volunteered that one time, when I met you."

"But you came back three more times, and you helped me find my donor."

"Yeah, about that." Ari shifted in his seat. "I figured that if I helped you, I could spend more time with you."

He looked over at me. "You do think I'm a jerk. Don't you?"

"No. Not at all," I said, feeling shy.

Then Ari reached over and held my hand, the one without the sandwich in it. We crossed the Mississippi River into Wisconsin and passed contoured cornfields that had been cleared for the winter, as though a giant comb had been pulled across the land. It was there, next to an open field, that I saw a black-and-white horse standing by a wooden fence, facing away from the cold wind. I knew it was just a horse, but today it held meaning. It was a sign, I decided, showing me the way. Today that horse was waiting there for me.

33

EAGAN

There weren't a lot of defining moments in my life. Lots of little moments, like when I saw a sunrise or a stunning view of the mountains, or when my dad carried me to bed, tucked me in, and read me a book. Or when Scott put his arm around me during a movie and I barely watched the show because I was more excited by him.

No doubt about it. The most important event of my life was my death. That day, that moment, seems to stand out above all the rest. Everything intensifies, slows down. I watch it in slow motion. I see the audience, the horror on their faces when I don't get up.

I feel bad for them. I mean, they're all left with that same image. Everyone there will remember that moment for the rest of their lives. For some, it will become one of the most important events of their own lives. It will change everything.

I've avoided thinking about how it is for everyone on Earth. I haven't had any desire to see my funeral. And I don't want to see any skating competitions without me in them. Maybe it's because I don't want to accept my own death.

I have a sudden ache to see Mom now, not just as a memory. I want to make sure she's okay, that she knows that I loved her even though we fought all the time. I want her to know that I'm sorry I left.

I wonder what she's doing now, whether she's still selling houses. Or has she become a recluse who stays in bed and never leaves her own house? I wonder if seeing my old pond skates on the back porch brings her pain or comfort.

I imagine her in my head. I see her dark, curly hair, cut just below her ears because she thought her ears stuck out otherwise. I see her manicured nails painted a rusty red color, the black-rimmed reading glasses she wore on her head. I see the way she puckered up her mouth when she drank lemonade, and the intense gaze of her watching me skate, as though she was on the ice with me.

And suddenly I'm back in my room. My own room with my comfy bed and pillows and the purple and white bedspread. Is this another memory? I didn't see this one flashing before me. So how did I get back? Was my death just a dream? Or did I wish this so hard that I made it happen?

Mom is here. She's going through my drawers. My green cashmere sweater is in her hands, the one I begged for when school started, even though it cost more than two pairs of jeans.

"Mom!" She doesn't answer. Can she hear me?

I'm an arm's length away. I step forward. The floor creaks, and I wonder if I made that noise. But our old house makes all kinds of noises.

Then Mom looks up, straight at me. But her eyes look right through me. She has dark circles under her bloodshot eyes. Her hair is longer than I remembered and it's uncombed. So unlike her. She looks as though she hasn't slept in a long time.

"Mom," I say again. But she doesn't hear me. She looks back at the sweater, brings it to her face, and inhales the scent. Tears stream down her face.

"I'm sorry, Mom." I'm crying too. "I never meant to leave you."

Then I notice her swollen belly under the blouse. Is she pregnant? At her age? What a shock! But I feel a sudden rush of joy. I'm going to have a baby brother or sister!

"Is that what you were going to tell me?"

Mom moves the sweater from her face and places it back in the drawer. Then she opens my desk drawer. A crumpled piece of paper sticks out. The letter she wrote me. She presses it open with her palm and reads it. Fresh tears flood her eyes and drip down onto the writing, smearing the ink.

Dear Eagan,

How did we get to this point? You're my whole life and I only want the best for you. That's why I'm hard on you. But please know that I love you more than anything else in the whole world. If I could take back that slap or anything else I ever did in my life that upset you, I would.

I can't, of course, so I don't expect you to just forgive and forget. I look forward to the day when we're not always at odds with each other. I had a difficult relationship with my own mother, and I was sure I would be different when I had children of my own. Sadly, it seems I have become all that I didn't want to be: my own mother. But my mother and I reconciled when you were born, and I hope you will one day be able to forgive me as well. I only hope I don't have to wait until I have grandchildren for that reconciliation to happen.

Love,
Mom

Thank God I saved that. I'd have hated for her to find the letter in the trash. That explains why we rarely visited Mom's parents, who lived eight hours away from us. Mom didn't get along with her own mother.

"Why?" she says, and her voice sounds like a wounded animal. "Why, why, why, why?"

I reach out to hold her, but my hands go right through her. How can I comfort her? How can I tell her I'm okay?

Am I really dead? If so, why do I feel so torn up inside? Why am I sobbing? Why do I feel so helpless?

"Mom," I shout through my tears. "I'm here!"

And as suddenly as I was thrown into the world, I'm torn out of it again. The gray mist swells around me and I hold my head, feeling dizzy. It's almost a relief to be back. Mom's grief was too much to bear.

"Where were you? Did you go back?" Miki asks me.

"In a way. I wanted to go back so much. But I didn't expect it to be so complicated."

Miki shakes her head. "That's just the beginning."

34

Amelia

Eagan lived in this town. Two months ago she'd walked up these steps. She'd slept in this house. And a couple of weeks ago she should have had Thanksgiving dinner with her family.

I looked up at the tidy, pale blue two-story house, older and smaller than ours. An autumn wreath hung on their door, with ribbons of brown and yellow trailing down. The neighbors had a giant Santa and Rudolph set up on the front lawn.

Ari looked at the decorations next door and the limp wreath on Eagan's house. "You sure you're up for this?"

I suddenly wished Mom was standing next to me. She'd always been with me whenever I faced something hard.

"Yes," I said with more confidence than I felt. I had to believe that if I'd come this far, there was a reason I was supposed to be here.

But my hands trembled. What could I possibly say to Eagan's family that would be any comfort at all?

I reached out and knocked on the door, which opened only seconds later. They must have seen us drive up.

A short, balding man opened the door. "Hi. Please come in." His voice was friendly.

He held the door for us and put out his hand to Ari. "I'm Mr. Lindeman, Eagan's dad," he said.

"I'm Ari," Ari said as he shook Mr. Lindeman's hand. "This is my friend Amelia."

"I'm so glad to meet you, Amelia," he said, holding my hand for a long moment. "We very much appreciated your letter."

Even through his sadness, I could see a kind face. My heart ached for him.

We faced the living room, which didn't look anything like I'd imagined from the outside of the house. The walls were the color of fresh melon. They had a white carpet and a white sofa. A plaid chair and ottoman matched the valance that covered pleated shades. It reminded me of a picture in one of those magazines that Mom liked to read.

Then my eyes settled on a guy standing just to the side of the entryway. He wore a red and white letter jacket with lots of patches on it.

"Hi," I said.

He looked hard at me. He was searching for a resemblance, but other than brown hair—and hers was much darker than mine—there was none.

Eagan's dad motioned him over.

"Scott, this is Amelia."

"Hi, Amelia." Scott shook my hand. I could tell by the way his hand held mine that he wasn't a relative of Eagan's. He was her boyfriend. My heart beat faster, as if taking all this in.

I was entranced by everything around me. I could sense Eagan's aura here, and it felt strangely familiar. My eyes settled on a wall of pictures—Eagan's life in chronological order: as a toddler in a snowsuit, with Santa, her first day of school. I walked over and stood in front of a picture of her at age eight in a sparkly skating outfit holding a trophy. She had wild, curly hair and brown, fiery eyes to match.

"Do you like to skate?" Scott asked behind me.

"I don't know how to skate."

"Oh." It sounded like I'd disappointed him.

"Would you like to see a video of Eagan?" Mr. Lindeman asked me.

"I'd love to."

"It's just excerpts from some of her competitions that we pulled together." He didn't say for what. For the funeral?

He put in a DVD and there she was, this beautiful girl, so full of life. I saw her strength, her skill, her poise, how easily she moved across the ice. She was so talented, so young. I heard her laugh on the tape. It was the kind of laugh that you knew was hard-kept, one that didn't happen too often. She spoke, and I swear I recognized her voice.

My eyes went wide when her friends called her Dynamo, the name I'd heard in my dream. I covered my mouth to keep in a shriek.

Mr. Lindeman stood up. "I'm just going to check on my wife, Cheryl. See what's keeping her."

"How are you feeling?" Ari asked when he left. "Are you tired?"

"A little," I confessed, not wanting to tear my eyes away from her image on the TV. "But I'm glad we came."

Scott's eyes were glued to the video as well. But during a

close-up of Eagan, he had to look away. I thought he might cry.

Muffled voices leaked down the stairway. One of the voices sounded angry. Ari shifted uncomfortably in his chair as if he was ready to bolt. Finally, Mr. Lindeman came back down. His face was flushed and he was wringing his hands.

He looked at me when he spoke. "I'm so sorry, Amelia. Cheryl has changed her mind. She feels it's just too soon."

He nodded at the TV, where Eagan was doing a sit spin. "Eagan was, well, she was the glue that held us together as a family. Cheryl has had such a hard time, and . . ." His voice broke and he looked down at his shoes.

"Maybe we should leave," Ari said.

Scott stood up. "Is it okay if I show her Eagan's room?"

Mr. Lindeman looked at the stairs. I thought he was going to say no. But then he nodded. "Of course."

I looked at Ari. "I'll wait here," he said.

I followed Scott up the stairs while Ari talked to Eagan's dad.

It was just like I knew it would be. The purple paint on her walls, the purple and white bedspread. Trophies and medals decorating her wall. Pictures of her with her friends on a bulletin board filled with skating programs and other memorabilia. One picture stood out. It was of Eagan and Scott. She looked stunning in a blue dress, and she had a white corsage on her wrist. Scott wore a black suit. His arm was around her waist. They were both smiling.

"You were her boyfriend," I said.

He nodded. "Yeah."

We stood there looking at each other. Scott was tall,

clean-cut, muscular, with short, dark hair. He was the kind of guy I suspect would date cheerleaders like Rachel.

"I don't know how to say this. I feel like Eagan's part of me. But I'm not *her*, you know?"

He nodded again. "I know."

"How long were you together?"

"Not long. A couple of months. But I loved her." He cleared his throat and looked away. "I should have been there. I was at my football banquet. Maybe my being there would have changed something. Maybe she wouldn't have fallen. Maybe she wouldn't have died."

He spun around when he realized what he'd just said. "I didn't mean . . ."

"It's okay," I assured him. I stared at the picture of them, of how happy they were. My heart fluttered in my chest, as if she was responding.

He put a finger on the picture. His eyes were watery. He sniffed twice. "I love you, babe," he whispered.

I felt like an intruder, so I looked at the opposite wall. There was something wrong with her room. Something not quite right. How could I know that when I'd never been here before?

Scott wiped a hand across his eyes. "It kinda helps to know that her heart is still beating."

"I'm glad you showed me her room." I turned to go then stopped. "Is this the way it always was? Did they move anything?"

"I was only here once. It looks the same as I remember it, though."

I wrapped my arms together as a shiver settled in my elbows. "I just thought there'd be something else here." I studied the room: a bed, two dressers, a desk and chair. "A chair," I said. "It's missing a chair."

Scott's face clouded. "What chair?"

I thought of the chair in my hospital room, the one that seemed so familiar. "A rocking chair."

Scott gasped. "Holy shit. Who told you about that?"

I put my hand over my heart. "No one. I just knew."

Scott closed the door to her room. "I never told them about it. The chair. Eagan was so mad, she said she didn't want her mom to have it. They never got along well. I thought it was what Eagan wanted, and then after a while, I couldn't tell them about it because they'd want to know why I hadn't said anything before."

"I don't understand."

"The rocking chair that Eagan and her grandpa made for her mom. It's hidden behind a panel in her closet."

"Why didn't her grandpa say anything?"

"He didn't know it was there."

We were interrupted then by shouting in the hallway. "You let her into Eagan's room? You had no right to do that."

"I think we better go," Scott said.

But I barely heard him. I couldn't move. Something was wrong. I sat down on Eagan's bed and leaned forward, doubled over by a sharp pain. It seared through me like razor blades cutting into my lower back. I felt dizzy, like I was going to black out.

"You okay? Amelia?"

Scott was yelling down the stairs, but I couldn't hear what he was saying. The light-headedness made his voice sound distant.

Ari was by my side. "It hurts, Ari."

"What's wrong?"

I thought I might vomit and pass out at the same time. I grabbed Ari's hand. I gasped. "It hurts," was all I could get out.

"I've called 911," a voice said.

I started to cry. "Am I going to die?"

Ari's voice was close. "Don't think about the pain. Concentrate on something else, Amelia."

Something else. All I could think about was that I was going to die after all I'd gone through, all the pain and stupid beeping machines. I was going to die on her bed. I'd failed her. Eagan was upset, so she was taking her heart back. God, don't let me die now.

I wanted to get away from the pain and dizziness, but I couldn't move. Couldn't talk. Couldn't even hear. I was caught in the spiral that was swirling around me, trapping me, killing me.

I wanted Mom and Dad more than ever. I wanted to tell them I loved them before I died.

Huge arms carried me. I was aware of people around me. A mask on my face. I felt something go through me, through my veins, seep up my arms. Then everything went black.

35

EAGAN

In one of my flashbacks, the tiniest thing happened during math class. Instead of closing my math book and picking it up like I was supposed to do, I pushed it off my desk onto the floor. It landed with a loud clunk. I stared at the book, at what I'd done, because in my memory that hadn't happened.

"I did it," I tell Miki. "I think I can change the past."

She stares at me with wide eyes. "You can't change things."

"But I already did. Okay, so it was something little, but if I could do that, then maybe I could go back to the accident and . . ."

"They're memories. They already happened. The world has already changed."

"What if I can change what happened?"

"You can't. You just thought you did."

"I can try."

"It's time for you to face the truth. I want you to see

something," she says. The fog opens up and we're in a hospital room.

A nurse works on a patient, inserting a needle, adjusting a tube, taking blood pressure.

Who is the patient? I hope it's not Grandpa.

Then I see a girl's form on the bed. For a brief instant I think it's me. Could it be? Maybe I'm not dead—maybe this has all been a dream, or I'm having one of those near-death experiences. Or am I like Scrooge? Was Miki sent to me to straighten me out before I turned into a real loser?

Whoever this girl is, she's hooked to a lot of machines. The room faces a nurse's station, and monitors beep out numbers above her head. That's it. I'm in a coma. I just thought I was dead.

Then I see her face. It isn't me. She looks so young—her face is pale. Is she dying too?

As I move to the side, I notice Miki standing next to me.

"Who is she?" I ask.

"She's a girl who had a heart transplant. But she's having some problems."

"Who was the donor?"

Miki looks at me.

"Oh." This really complicates things.

"You can come in now," the nurse tells someone in the hall. A woman walks in. She has one of those green hospital masks over her face, but I can see a smile in her eyes, and I recognize the worry behind the smile. She takes the girl's hand with her gloved one. I move in for a closer look.

The girl has light brown hair, straight and fine. She looks

younger than me, but there's a wisdom in her face, as though she's older than her age.

"Mom?" Her voice is rough. "I'm sorry."

She sighs. "Why didn't you tell me, Amelia?"

Tears run down Amelia's face. "I should have. I didn't know how."

The woman reaches out a gloved finger and wipes away a tear. "It wasn't a rejection. You had a reaction to the buildup of cyclosporine in your system. It caused a bad urinary tract infection. They switched your med to tacrolimus. They have it under control now. You're out of danger."

"Promise?"

Her mom moves closer and takes Amelia's hand. I think she's going to put it on Amelia's heart, my heart, but she places it on her own and puts both her hands on top of Amelia's hand. "I promise. With all my heart."

The girl sniffs. "Speaking of promises, don't blame Ari. I made him do it. Now he probably hates me."

Her mom's mouth turns into a smirk. "Oh, I doubt that. He's outside waiting to see you."

"He's here? Can I see him?"

"I'll send him in."

A boy enters. He looks about my age. The mask on his face squishes his dark hair against his neck. His dark brown eyes are bloodshot.

I sense Amelia's shyness, hear the familiar beat of my heart in her chest. I'm in awe of my heart inside her, keeping her alive. I feel the heart, my heart, flutter.

"I thought I was going to die," she says.

He moves closer and takes her hand. "But you didn't."

"No. I didn't."

"You got it out of the way," he says softly. "Now you can get on with your life."

"Are you talking about the rejection scare or meeting her family?" she asks.

"Both," he says.

The girl's face screws up like she's going to cry again. "Eagan's mom didn't want to meet me, Ari. She hates me."

He squeezes her hand. "Give her time. At least you made the effort."

———⋀⋁———

Figures. Mom wouldn't even see her. I'm irritated with Mom even though a moment ago I was crying for her. "Is she going to be okay?" I ask as I watch them.

Miki shrugs. "I don't know. I hope so."

"What? You don't know? Then what are we doing here?"

"You wanted to change the past. You should know what you'd change."

I get it. I had my shot at life. Now it's someone else's turn. I let out a long sigh. "I guess I can't go back after all."

"You never really could," Miki says.

———⋀⋁———

"Amelia," the boy says. "You've got quite a crowd outside. Your dad is out there, and that guy Scott is waiting to see you. Didn't you tell him you already have a boyfriend?"

Her pale face takes on a bit of color. "Did you just say you were my boyfriend?"

He reaches over and squeezes her hand. "If that's okay with you. I mean, if your parents will ever let me see you again."

"You're not just saying that to make me feel better?"

"I'm saying it because the first time I saw you in the hospital, I wanted to come back the very next day. But I was afraid you'd think I was stalking you. I mean, I wouldn't drive my beater to Wisconsin for just anyone."

A blush works its way onto her cheeks. "I wonder what Scott wants."

"I don't know, but I'm glad he's not competition because, to be honest, I think he could beat the crap out of me. That dude is built."

I let out a scream. "Oh my God! Scott's here?"

Miki twirls around in her yellow dress. "See? You thought you'd never see him again."

The boy, Ari, leaves, and a moment later Scott walks in. I've been so immersed in my life, it only seems like a moment ago that I saw him. So the first thing I notice is that he's lost weight. Instead of filling out his letter jacket, it hangs from his frame. Not that he isn't still gorgeous. But he carries himself differently. He walks like someone who's suffered a serious defeat. I'd love to give him a big kiss underneath that hospital mask.

He stands away from the bed and holds a bouquet of white roses in a pink vase. "How are you feeling?"

"Stupid. Scared. The doctors said I had a chemical reaction, a buildup of the cyclosporine. They switched me to another drug. I'm feeling a lot better already. I can't believe this happened at her house. I thought Eagan was trying to tell me something. Maybe she just wanted me to go away."

Scott sets the vase down on the nightstand. "I'm sorry you got sick, but I'm glad you came. I think she was trying to tell *me* something. I mean, you knew about the chair."

The girl takes a deep breath. "That was unreal."

Scott sticks his hands into his pockets. "I told her parents about the chair. I should have told them sooner. It was this secret Eagan and I shared, and I guess I didn't want to let it go. It was something just the two of us knew, and that made it special. But I figured if you knew about the chair, then maybe Eagan wanted them to have it after all."

The chair. I'd forgotten about it. "How sweet." I sniff back a tear. "Scott was keeping the rocking chair safe for me. But they should have it. Besides, Mom will need it for the new baby."

Miki nods.

Strange how I have a need to make Mom and Dad feel better. My former self might not have. Who knew that death would make me a better person?

"Well, the nurse said not to stay long. One visitor at a time. And your dad is waiting to see you. I just wanted to say that seeing you made me feel a connection," Scott said.

"I know what you mean. I feel like she's part of me now, and I'm going to live for both of us."

He turns toward the door. "Believe me, Amelia. You got a strong heart. It's not going to give out on you."

"Thanks for the flowers, Scott."

He leaves. Amelia sighs and closes her eyes. I want to follow Scott, but something is keeping me here.

"She needs to talk to your mom," Miki says.

"How can I help her? Nobody can see or hear me. I can't talk to anyone."

"Wanna bet?" she says.

"But how?" I ask.

"I'll show you." And she pulls me away.

Ask anyone who's died and you'll get the same answer: the best way to talk to someone still living is in their dreams.

My parents waited for me in their dreams, hoping that if they found me, they could somehow keep me from leaving again. Dreams let them pretend. So much easier than facing real life.

Mom had dreamed of me as a little girl. In that dream I was still alive, and she was upset when she woke up and realized I was dead. It was as if she'd lost me all over again. That dream led to uncontrollable sobbing in the middle of the night.

I came in the faint early morning light after she'd had a restful night's sleep and was ready to hear what I had to say. Her mind was unusually clear. Mom's arm was tucked under her pillow and her brown hair was disheveled. She'd kicked off the bedspread earlier and now had drawn her body into a fetal position in search of warmth.

In this dream she knew I had died. She was sitting at the kitchen table and she saw me as I looked the day of the accident. I had on my warm-up pants and a sweatshirt.

I stood at the other side of the table, my hand resting on the back of the chair. I was quiet until I knew she'd seen me. I didn't want to scare her.

"Hi, Mom."

She looked hard at me, not sure she could trust her eyes. "Eagan? Is that really you?"

I nodded.

"How could you leave me like that?" She said it as if I'd broken her heart on purpose.

"It's not like I wanted to leave," I said.

She shook her head, both in her dream and in real life on her pillow. "I need you," she said with tears in her eyes.

"I'm sorry, Mom," I said in a softer voice. "You'll have another child. She'll be a comfort to you until you see me again."

"But she won't replace you."

"Good," I said. "I wouldn't want her to."

Then I changed form. I don't know how I did it. Maybe because it was a dream and in dreams you have that ability. I became that other girl, Amelia. Mom stared at me. Her eyes widened in panic. "Eagan!"

"I'm right here, Mom."

She stared at me, at this other girl I'd become who had the same voice as her daughter's.

"You're not my daughter."

"No. But maybe Amelia can show you where I am." I paused. "I love you, Mom."

"I love you."

"I don't fear the worst anymore. It's all good."

Then Mom dreamed about the baby, whispering softly to her about her big sister. I could tell Mom was going to wake up differently this time. No more sobbing. She'd remember this dream and would keep it close to her heart.

I waved as I faded from her dream. "Be happy, Mom."

Mom nodded at the thought, and she smiled at me, both in her dream and on her pillow.

36

Amelia

I stared out the window at the Milwaukee skyline. If I leaned just right, I could see Lake Michigan. The whitecaps reminded me of the froth on the top of a root beer. I had on the same jeans and shirt I'd worn to Eagan's house. It had felt weird to lie in bed with my clothes on. But I didn't want to sit in the chair. So I perched on the edge of the bed, waiting for Mom and Dad to take me home.

They were downstairs talking to reporters at a press conference that the hospital had set up. It was national news that I'd had an episode at the home of my donor. Reporters kept coming to the ward, asking to see me. Dad said that someone from CNN had called. Mom kept them all away. I just wanted to be left alone.

My levels are good now. The danger has passed. What if I'd died in her house, right on Eagan's bed? Now that *really* would have been news.

How would the reporters react if I told them how she'd

changed me? Would they believe that Eagan gave me a sense of humor and a feisty mouth that seemed to spill out thoughts that came from nowhere? Would they believe that she'd told me her nickname was Dynamo? That I knew she was a figure skater? That I knew about the rocking chair she'd hidden in her closet?

As I watched the waves splashing against the shore, I remembered watching the video of Eagan on the ice, her body effortlessly flying through the air. I'd heard her laugh, watched her move with a confidence I couldn't imagine having. She might have died, but at least she knew how to live.

All I had were my drawings. Pages of that magnificent horse from my dream, the one who'd led me here. I'd tried over and over to capture the image on paper, but each effort came up short.

Someone behind me cleared her throat. I turned around, thinking the discharge nurse had more instructions. But a woman stood just inside the door.

"May I come in?" she asked. I recognized Eagan's mom from pictures at her house. She was short but carried herself in an upright, almost regal stance. Her curly hair was pinned up. She smiled at me, but her pointed chin and high cheekbones made her seem less inviting than the smile intended.

My heart skipped a beat. "Mrs. Lindeman?"

She walked to the other side of the bed. "You're going home today?"

I nodded. My throat felt dry.

"That's wonderful. We've been praying for you."

Was she here because she felt guilty? She seemed so

restrained, like I imagined the Queen of England would be if I met her. It was then that I noticed her round belly.

"You're pregnant," I blurted out.

She put a hand on her stomach. "Yes. I'm due in April."

I shook my head. "Eagan didn't know."

Mrs. Lindeman took a step back. "How did you know that?"

"I don't know," I stammered. "I just knew."

She tilted her head to one side and softly rubbed her stomach. "I tried to tell Eagan the day she died."

That was something I *didn't* know.

"Scott told me about the chair. He said you knew about that too."

"Yes," I said in a whisper.

"I had a dream the other night," she said. "Eagan was there. It was . . . strange. When I awoke, I wasn't sure if I'd dreamed it or if it really happened."

I knew all about strange dreams.

"She came to me in the dream. But she looked different."

I held my breath and closed my eyes as a cinnamon and rust–colored horse galloped through my mind. "What did she look like?"

Mrs. Lindeman walked around the bed and stood in front of me, studying me. "She looked like a girl I didn't recognize. It wasn't until I got up close that I realized she was my daughter. I thought, 'How silly.' How could a mother not recognize her own daughter? Then she spoke to me. I heard her voice, but it was coming from this other girl."

"Who?" I whispered. Her eyes held so much grief that it was hard to look at her. Was that how my mom would have looked if I'd died?

"You. She looked just like you."

I blew out a breath, letting her words sink in. "I'm so sorry," I finally said, because there was nothing else I could say. I wished I could take away that pain. I held back the tears in my own eyes as hers flowed down her cheeks. Could she ever forgive me for taking her daughter's heart?

Mr. Lindeman was at the door. He watched his wife from behind her, his hands held out in a way that looked as if he was ready to run and catch her if she collapsed.

She sighed. "We had a . . . difficult relationship. I'm not sure she always knew how much I loved her.

"She was strong," she said. "Not only physically. She had this focus when skating that was amazing. I don't know how she made that mistake and hit her head. But Eagan always knew something the rest of us didn't. I believe she knew she'd die young."

Mrs. Lindeman put her hand out and leaned forward, hesitant. "May I listen?"

I nodded.

She touched my heart for a few seconds, then put her ear on my chest and listened. The fragrance of her stiff hair spray and her soapy skin smell made my heart quicken. After a moment she pulled back, cocked her head, and nodded as though she recognized the beat.

"Yes," she said. "That's her heartbeat."

She looked up at me. "I'm sorry I couldn't see you sooner after you drove all that way." She kissed her palm and laid it on my heart again. "And I'm sorry for any pain I caused you, my darling."

Finally, she reached out to me. I hugged her, feeling the

weight of her growing child press into me. The tears that I'd been holding back came anyway.

When she let go, Mr. Lindeman pulled his wife into his arms. She sobbed silently. "Eagan knew that you loved her, Cheryl," he assured her in a quiet voice. "She always knew."

I was released from the hospital later that afternoon, and we headed home to Minnesota shortly after that. I leaned back in the seat and closed my eyes as the Milwaukee suburbs thinned out to farmland.

I'd thought Eagan had sent me here to help her mom get through her grief. But maybe it was for me. I had to learn to accept her precious gift. I was learning to bear the guilt over the fact that someone else's tragedy had become my good fortune. And there was a price to that good fortune. I'd always feel a responsibility to make my life worthwhile.

Someday I'd come back for another visit. Mrs. Lindeman had invited me. She'd given me a picture of Eagan. But when I got better, the first thing I planned to do was to learn how to skate and ride horses.

Mom and Dad talked softly in the front seat. Their voices felt like a warm blanket, reassuring and comforting. Soon I was asleep.

I was galloping across a grassy pasture on the horse from my dream. Eagan was with me. This time she was right behind me, holding on to my waist as we rode together.

I was leading us now, on this magnificent horse that I knew I'd spend years trying to capture on paper. I would draw us on the horse, riding through woods and prairies and over high mountains and into the future.

My eyelids fluttered as I heard Mom's voice carry to the backseat. "I can't believe the nerve of that reporter at the press conference. He asked me if we'd known all the problems in store for Amelia, would we still have gone through with the transplant."

"What'd you say?" Dad asked.

But it was me who answered him. "In a heartbeat."

37

EAGAN

Miki takes my hand. "We're ready for you now."

"Ready?" I glance at my life. The fog is a mere shadow in the distance. There's a small cloud hanging over my head, a leftover remnant. I look up at it.

Miki motions toward the hill. "I have a surprise." She looks as if she wants to blow at the cloud, as though she could break it up with a single breath.

She leads me over the hill to, of all things, a skating rink. The rink is as smooth as glass, like after a Zamboni slide. I bend down to touch it. Not too hard, like so many of the hockey rinks I'd skated on. This one has some give to it.

Best of all, there are no boards around the rink, just a flat edging that stretches out to stands full of people. So many people!

I look down. I'm still wearing my competition dress, the same plum-colored one with the sparkling rhinestones, and it's no longer gray. I'm also wearing my skates. My hair feels tight against my head. I know what I'm supposed to do. I mean, I may be dead, but I'm not dense.

A woman in the front row of the audience waves at me. "Eagan. Over here."

It's Grandma, but she hardly resembles the grandma I remember, the one I visited in the hospital, who was thin and worn-out and so wrinkly. Her silver hair curls around her shoulders, and her cheeks are pink and vibrant. She's wearing that same purple dress that she was buried in. I skate over to her.

She embraces me and tears fill her eyes. "I've missed you. You're so grown-up and beautiful!"

Grandma still smells like her favorite perfume, Chanel No. 5.

"Is it really you, Grandma?"

"Do you remember when I brought you to skating practice when you were nine? How I kept screaming because I thought the other skaters were going to run into you?"

"Yeah. You said we looked like go-carts going in a million different directions."

She hugs me again. "It's me, darling. And I can't wait to see you skate again."

"Grandma, there's something you should know. The last time I skated I actually *did* run into something: the wall."

She pats my outfit. "No matter. I'm sure you'll do just fine today."

Okay. No pressure. I skate to the middle and take my pose. I close my eyes as I wait for the music to start, gathering my focus toward the execution of a program I've practiced so much it's ingrained into every cell of my body. This is a gift, a chance to do it right, and there is no way I want to mess up again.

It's dark except for a spotlight circling me. The music starts and I turn and skate. I don't have to think now. I skate a pass around the rink and throw my double combination. A burst of applause fills the rink. I put out my arms and position my fingers. Every move aligns with the music, as though it's connected.

My double axel is next. I push off, and I know in that instant of pushing off that I will land it. And I do. More cheers and applause.

The corner is approaching, the one where I launch my triple lutz, the jump where you're turned backward and you can't see the boards. Even though I know there aren't any boards in this rink, I'm nervous. This was the jump that killed me.

So I think about how I landed that jump in warm-ups the night I died. I remember landing it hundreds of times in practice. And I let go of all the fear and doubt. I let my body do what it knows how to do. I throw the most graceful triple lutz in the history of skating. I know because I feel it when I'm rotating, when I'm in the air, and when I land and bring my arms up.

The crowd erupts.

I make the rest of my jumps and my spins. And before I know it, my program is over. I curtsy to the cheering audience. They give me a standing ovation.

"Thank you," I say, and wave at them all.

Grandma is clapping hard. "That's my granddaughter!" she yells.

"You were wonderful." Miki has a huge smile that radiates from her shining face.

"Thanks." Grandma comes over and hugs me, and behind

her is Mr. Swanson, who used to live across the street from us. I see other people who look familiar. They're all dead, of course. But they're not ashen gray, and now, neither am I.

The gray fog is behind me now, like a storm that's passed. As we exit the stadium, the people head down the grassy hill toward a bright light, talking excitedly. I put my hand up to block the brightness penetrating my eyes, but it doesn't seem to bother anyone else. A man picks a flower along the way. Another flower pops up in the same space.

Grandma is beside me. "Are you ready?" she asks.

That perfect voice calls out to us in song. The bright light is now a yellow haze. The people ahead of me fade into its golden rays.

I look back to where my life had been.

It's always risky to think of letting go. That's why this is the perfect ending. Nothing left to reconcile. I skated my best program yet. I just wish my friends and family could have seen me. At least Grandma was here.

"I'm ready," I say, and the three of us hold hands: me, Grandma, and Miki.

"My two girls," Grandma says with a catch in her voice.

It occurs to me then that I might have known Miki before. "Did I know you when I was alive?" I ask her.

She flashes a knowing grin. "In a way. We have a lot in common." Then she lets go of my hand and dances toward the light just ahead of us. She has a natural gracefulness about her. She'd make a good skater.

"I don't feel dead," I tell Grandma.

"You're not. You're alive in a different way than before."

The meadow blends into the radiant softness. "This better be good."

Grandma squeezes my hand. "Trust me. It is."

I think of Mom and Dad, Grandpa, Kelly, Jasmine, Scott, and all my friends. I remember Amelia, the girl my heart saved, the same heart that led her back to Mom for me. She doesn't know it, but we saved each other.

"Don't worry. You're not leaving them," Grandma says. "We always watch over those we love."

"Do you think they know that?"

Grandma smiles and raises one eyebrow. "Not if we're careful."

ACKNOWLEDGMENTS

If you think a book is a solitary effort, take a look at the following list. I owe a deep debt of gratitude to them all:

To Gary Gustafson and Seth Jacobson, who shared their transplant stories with me, and to Sara Anderson and Erin Ellsworth for referring them to me; to Ann Eidson and the St. Paul Figure Skating Club; to Maria Sperduto, Katie Berry, Roxanne and Rachel Rice, Lynn Christie, and Alana and Jillian, for imparting their skating experiences, teaching me the lingo, and helping me with all things skating related; to Monica Barnes for being my constant pillar. To my wonderful agent, Mary Cummings, for believing in this story as much as I did (maybe more), and to her associate, Betsy Amster. To my editor extraordinaire, Emily Easton, and her associate editor, Stacy Cantor, for shining the light, and to the wonderful staff at Walker for everything.

To Jane Resh Thomas and my Hamline University advisors—Carolyn Coman, Ron Koertge, Marsha Wilson Chall, and Marsha Qualey—their handprints are all over my manuscript. To the faculty and students in the MFA in the Writing for Children Program at Hamline University for their encouragement. And a special thank-you to Ann Schulman for her help and to the Pheasant writing group for their willingness to listen to crummy first drafts.

I hope I didn't forget anyone. Any mistakes in this manuscript are completely my own.

AUTHOR NOTE

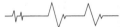

I began this book shortly after my mother died of congestive heart failure and my nephew Jason was killed in a motorcycle accident. It started out as therapy—it kept me writing through my grief. Jason was an organ donor. I liked the idea that part of him still lived on in the world, not only in our memories, but in some unique way in those lives he touched as an organ donor.

The theory of cellular memory suggests that memories are stored not only in the brain, but also in our cells. Although most scientists reject the notion of cellular memory, Dr. Paul Pearsall, a clinical neuropsychologist at the University of Hawaii and a member of the heart transplant study team at the University of Arizona, interviewed 150 individuals who had received a heart transplant. He found that many of the transplant recipients had acquired characteristics of their heart donors following surgery.

Dr. Pearsall reported that one of the recipients was an eight-year-old girl who received the heart of another girl who'd been murdered. After the transplant, the recipient had nightmares of a man murdering her. The psychiatrist she saw reported that the images were so specific that they notified the police. She described the man, the place of the murder, and the weapon. They found the murderer based on her evidence.

In her book *Change of Heart*, Claire Sylvia, a dancer, wrote about her heart and lung transplant and how she acquired the characteristics and cravings of her eighteen-year-old donor, including his favorites, beer and chicken nuggets, which she'd never had a taste for before.

So much is still not understood about the connection between the heart and brain. Although none of the recipients I questioned had experienced this phenomenon, it raises interesting questions. And as a writer, I find there's no better place to explore these questions than in fiction. I hope you've enjoyed my story.